ASSASSINS ROGUE

AN ENGLISH ASSASSINS SPY THRILLER

RACHEL AMPHLETT

SAXON
PUBLISHING

CHAPTER ONE

Flight Lieutenant Kelly O'Hara would live for another forty-eight hours.

Right now, she was preoccupied with finding the packet of cigarettes she swore blind she had tucked into her pocket upon entering the van that collected them from the base last night.

She patted her breast pocket, then checked her trousers before uttering a string of curses.

'Want a smoke?'

Turning at the sound of a male voice, Kelly rolled her eyes and stuck a hand on her hip as her colleague Josh Connor sauntered towards her.

'Cheeky bastard – those are mine. Is nothing sacred around here?'

'Your lungs.' He grinned, and launched the packet at her.

Catching it in a practised grip, Kelly pulled out a cigarette and accepted the lighter Josh held out. 'You sound like my mother.'

'Perish the thought.'

'Where's Marie?' she said, exhaling smoke to the side before making sure the packet went back in her pocket, not his.

Josh jerked his head towards the door of the building that resembled a large corrugated steel Portacabin. 'Wanted a word with the chief.'

'Christ.'

Kelly turned her attention to the setting sun, and breathed a trail of nicotine-laden smoke skywards.

The concrete landing strip in front of her provided an uninterrupted view across a wide vista.

An indigo tint darkened the fringes of the horizon while half a dozen small bats dived upon the insects hovering close to the hedgerows bordering the open space on the western edge.

An eerie silence had descended on the flat landscape. No birds called from the copse of trees behind the temporary building, no shouted commands carried across the airfield.

Compared to their home base, the place was a ghost field, similar to one of the crumbling World War Two bomber airfields that remained in the English countryside.

A countryside that was at least a five-hour flight

from whatever Eastern European hiding place they had been ushered to in haste last night.

Kelly sighed, took another drag on the cigarette and rolled her neck muscles, easing the tiredness from her arms after a twelve-hour shift, and watched as the sun began to drop below the beech trees half a mile away.

Silhouetted against the quivering orange blush on the horizon stood the aircraft she had been flying, all thirty-six feet of it.

A MQ-9A Reaper, to be exact.

A drone.

'When are they taking us back home?'

'I'm not sure.' Josh scuffed at the dirt path running alongside the landing strip. 'The chief said they've got some post-operational discussions to have, and then he'll arrange for the car to take us over to the main hangar to save us the walk. I reckon we'll be flown out of here before midnight.'

He squinted through the cigarette smoke to a large tumbledown hangar at the farthest edge of the field. 'I could murder a beer after that. Do you think they've got a bar here?'

Kelly wrinkled her nose. 'I don't think they've got *anything* here. I mean, look at this place. What did he call it?'

'He didn't say.' He shrugged. 'I didn't catch the name if he did. Too much else to take in, to be honest. I was concentrating more on the mission briefing.'

'Yeah, me too.'

'Probably won't tell us anyway. He did say this one was top secret, hence all the paperwork we had to sign on the way here.'

'True.'

Kelly wasn't overly concerned by the secrecy – it would still be noted on her service record and maybe, just maybe, add a little more weight to her credentials when she sought promotion at the end of the year.

Because it was one thing to be the Reaper's pilot, but quite another to be the one in the background, calling the shots.

Giving the command to strike.

Six hours ago, that had been the chief's decision.

Colonel Paul Richards had remained at her shoulder while the Reaper glided over mountains and rivers, crossed an inland sea and bore down on the Middle Eastern territory that was the aircraft's final destination.

He stayed there for the entire flight, watching the screens, murmuring encouragement from time to time, and updating Marie on incoming intelligence about their target's progress on the ground from a small group of resources who would do anything for cash.

'Who is he?' Josh had asked at one point, glancing up from his constant monitoring of the Reaper's sensors.

The chief had shrugged.

Kelly had glared at Josh – the target's identity was

none of their business – but the chief had answered after a time.

'Just another terrorist to deal with, before it's too late.'

Satisfied, Josh had returned to his screens and fallen silent while Kelly had called in their approach.

The crew took no pleasure in what they did. It was a job, that was all, but a split second before the AGM-114 Hellfire missile found its target, Marie had let out a shocked gasp that made Kelly look up from her instrument panel.

The woman had turned white as she'd watched the black four-by-four vehicle explode thousands of metres below their cameras, her hands shaking as she reacted to Kelly's barked command to stay focused, to bring the Reaper safely home.

A clatter shook Kelly from her thoughts and she turned to see Marie Weston, mission intelligence coordinator, push her way out through the Portacabin door, her boots clanging on the metal steps leading down to the stony soil where they stood waiting as the door crashed closed behind her.

The thirty-year-old had been quieter than usual once the Reaper had taxied to a standstill and Kelly had killed the engines, and now a shocked stare filled her eyes.

Kelly crushed the remains of her cigarette under her boot, blew the smoke away from the other woman's face and peered at her.

'What happened in there?'

Marie didn't stop when she reached them. She grasped each of them by the arm and dragged them with her, away from the Portacabin, away from where the Reaper waited for its next mission.

'We can't say here,' she managed, her breath short. 'We've got to get out of here.'

Her eyes darted left, then right, then over her shoulder.

'What's going on?' said Josh. 'You all right?'

'No, I'm not all right.' Marie's pace quickened. 'There's a gap in the hedge over there, see? We can squeeze through it – with any luck there's a road or something nearby. We might be able to get a lift off a local, or someone.'

Kelly frowned at the desperation clawing at the woman's words, and pulled her to a standstill. 'Marie? What's going on?'

Marie's eyes found the Portacabin, then Kelly once more. 'Have you ever seen Colonel Richards before?'

'No.'

'Have you heard of him?'

'No,' said Kelly, then smiled. 'But there's a lot of top brass I haven't met before.'

'Did either of you check his credentials? His background?'

Kelly fished out her mobile phone. 'No, but then there's no mobile signal anyway. Besides, we haven't stopped since we got picked up last night and flown here.'

'Exactly.' Marie turned away and began to walk again.

Josh held up his hands to Kelly, and she shrugged before nudging him forward.

'We've been used,' said Marie once they'd caught up with her.

'What do you mean, used?' Josh shoved his hands in his pockets, his height giving him an advantage over the two women. He reached the gap in the hedge before them and paused. 'Used by who?'

'I don't know,' said Marie. She looked as if she was going to cry. 'But it wasn't a terrorist in that car. I saw his face. He looked out of the window just before the missile hit. I saw his face.'

Josh's eyes opened wide. 'You mean you recognised him?'

Marie nodded, her expression distraught.

'Who was it?' said Kelly, keeping her voice calm despite her heart hammering, a sudden rush to her head that made it difficult to hear, as if she had just dived underwater.

'Jeffrey Dukes.'

'Who?'

'He's the special adviser to Robert Nivens. The Foreign Secretary,' said Marie. 'He's been in the papers on and off for the past three months.'

Kelly swallowed. When she looked at Josh, he was staring at Marie with his mouth open in shock.

'Are you sure?' she managed.

'I'm sure. When I asked the chief—'

'Wait, *that's* what you were talking to him about? Why would you—'

Josh's words were cut short as Marie let out a scream.

When Kelly turned to face him, he was no longer there.

Confused, she took a step back, her mind trying to process the fact that her crew mate now lay on his back in the grass, a bloody entry hole in his torso.

He uttered a final gurgling breath, and then his head slumped to one side.

The second shot narrowly missed her cheek, but she felt its searing hot presence as it caressed her hair.

'Move!'

Marie's scream galvanised her into a sprint, terror and confusion marring disbelief that this was happening, that Marie was right, that Josh was dead.

Another whip crack overhead shattered any illusion that someone had shot him in error, and she ducked as the tree trunk beside her exploded.

Raising her hand to protect her face from the splinters that showered her, Kelly grimaced as she stumbled over uneven ground, the terrain dipping and undulating under her boots.

Marie wasn't slowing down – the intelligence officer tore through the undergrowth, vaulting fallen branches as she led the way down a hill.

Kelly could see a track at the bottom, a single ribbon of pebbles and dirt splitting the forest in two, and then collided with her crew mate when she stopped beside a fallen tree, hands on her knees as she gulped for breath.

'Which way?'

'I don't know.' Marie spun on her heel at the sound of voices at the top of the embankment and pulled Kelly into a crouching position.

In the distance a vehicle engine carried on the breeze, its driver clunking through the gears as he negotiated the twisting route.

Kelly strained her ears to listen. It was coming from below the airfield, not from it.

And it would pass right under their position.

'We need to stop that vehicle. It could be our only way out of here.'

Marie clenched her jaw. 'Listen, we know we're in Eastern Europe, right?'

'Probably.'

'Okay. There's a place I know about. They'll help us.'

Kelly listened while her intelligence officer rattled off the details, her thoughts spinning. 'Wait, how do you know this?'

'I just do.' Marie clutched hold of her arm, her

fingers digging into the muscles. 'We have to split up, Kel. You need to go.'

'Are you sure? Where are you going?'

'I'll meet you there, but I'll make my way down to a village, or find a house – something. I'll get help once I'm there.'

'What if something happens to you?'

Her colleague's eyes hardened. 'We have to tell someone what happened back there. We stand a better chance if we split up. Remember the code words, all right? They won't help you otherwise.'

Marie rose and took off at a sprint, her boots snapping twigs as her figure disappeared amongst the trees until all that was left was the sound of Kelly's breathing.

Panicked breathing, gasping breaths as she forced herself to move and half-ran half-tumbled down the slope towards the road and the sound of the engine.

She slid to a halt beside the thick trunk of an ancient oak, dappled sunlight turning its leaves, and peered around it.

Please don't let it be them.

A rusting hulk of an ancient pick-up truck rumbled towards her, the suspension creaking as it negotiated potholes, puddles and deep ruts in the dirt track.

A single man was behind the wheel, his grizzly features more apparent as the vehicle drew closer…

Kelly stepped out from behind the tree and waved

her hands above her head, moving to the middle of the track and blocking its path.

When the pick-up truck eased to a standstill, she moved to the driver's window, and his brow creased as he lowered it.

'Do you speak English?'

'A little, yes.'

'I'm sorry – I don't know where I am.'

'Dzerzhinsk.'

'I meant, which country?'

The driver blinked. 'Belarus.'

Belarus?

The driver was looking at her with an inquisitiveness bordering on suspicion.

Kelly forced a grim smile. 'I'll kill that boyfriend of mine when I find him. We got lost, hiking.'

He stared at her, his eyes running up and down the green overalls she wore.

She shrugged, held his gaze.

'Ah. Do you want to wait here for him?' he said, an eyebrow cocked.

'No.' She heard the fear in her voice, forced another smile. 'He's got the car keys. He can find his own way back.'

The driver threw back his head and laughed. 'He doesn't deserve you.'

'Damn right.'

'Get in.'

'Thanks.' She drew the seatbelt over her chest and exhaled.

'Where are you headed?'

Kelly swallowed, peered in the door mirror, and then urged the driver to get going.

'Prague.'

CHAPTER TWO

Prague, Czech Republic

The bookshop provided a splash of colour against the grey sombre buildings crowding it on either side.

A light over its front door cast a soft glow over the uneven cobblestones, despite the early hour. In the window was a selection of maps and guidebooks for the tourists and, for the more discerning customer, first editions and other rare tomes.

A sandwich board on the footpath teased the titles of the more intriguing titles on offer, fat raindrops attacking the white and blue chalk lettering and obliterating the top of the Czech koruna symbol in front of the prices.

Nathan Crowe dried his glasses with the corner of

his thin sweatshirt, held them up to the light above the till to check for smears, then replaced them and ran a hand through unruly brown hair.

'Shit,' he murmured as he looked down and saw the small puddle forming by his feet.

The rainstorm would put paid to any passing tourist traffic this morning – visitors to the city tended to stay close to their hotels when the weather was inclement instead of exploring the myriad back streets further east along the river.

Nathan sighed, wandered to the back of the shop and found a towel hanging from a hook in the kitchenette he'd installed a year ago after growing tired of walking upstairs to the flat every time he wanted a hot drink.

Drying his hair, he slapped the switch on the kettle and resigned himself to a morning of stock-taking.

Once a mug of Earl Grey tea stood steaming next to the till, its sweet bergamot aroma filling the air, he turned his attention to the day's tasks. His eyes fell upon the row of six boxes stacked against a wall beyond an archway leading from the bookstore, and he smiled.

Despite the work, he looked forward to finding out if there were any more hidden gems amongst the dusty and spineless offerings cluttering the first box he'd peered into last night.

The delivery was made by Mr Svoboda's grandson late on Saturday afternoon. As he owned the largest car in the family, it had fallen to him to dispose of his grandfather's belongings after the old man had been moved to a care home.

Nathan had spotted a couple of first editions within the collection, offered a fair price and seen Mr Svoboda's grandson on his way, the man returning to his car with a bounce in his stride.

Thunder rolled overhead, and Nathan turned to see the rain striking the cobblestones with renewed fervour, commuters hurrying past with their umbrellas held aloft.

Not one of them paused to look at this morning's display.

He sighed, then moved to the first box and pulled back the lid.

Cradling eight hardbacks minus their original covers, he walked back to the computer, entered the details into stock, and then crossed to the shelves filling the space.

Once a thriving private bank, the building had changed hands several times over the centuries since being built. The first record of it becoming a bookshop was in the early nineties, although it had lain empty for a decade prior to that while the Soviet bloc around it dissolved.

As Nathan moved between the rows of shelves, his fingers traced gold leaf titles worn thin by age and authors' names who had faded into obscurity for all but the shrewdest collector.

Three books were left in his hands when footsteps

sounded on the patterned slate tiles that led from the cobblestones to the bookshop's threshold.

He glanced up from his work. 'Morning.'

A woman, dressed in faded jeans and wearing a short coat caught his eye before he turned back to the shelves.

She hadn't acknowledged his greeting.

Perhaps she didn't realise that his Czech was terrible and his German not much better, which was why he stumbled along in English for most transactions.

A smile twitched at the corner of his mouth in sympathy.

Wet strands of hair clung to the woman's face, tendrils escaping from a short ponytail and plastered to her skin by the rain. He placed two more books on a shelf next to a collection of Charles Dickens' works. Perhaps she would like a hot drink while she browsed.

Still, she had said nothing.

He tried again. 'Morning.'

The woman wore a hunted expression as her eyes darted to the door, then back to where he stood.

Nathan lowered the book he was holding, and frowned. 'Can I help you?'

'I hope so.' Her voice was soft, but abrupt – as if used to staccato responses. She took a tentative step towards him. 'Do you have a 1915 first edition of *The Thirty-Nine Steps* by John Buchan?'

He swallowed.

'I'm not sure there's an edition from that year available,' he managed.

The woman's face fell. 'I was told if I came here, and asked for that book, you could help me.'

He could hear the desperation in her voice, and yet—

'Let me have a look behind the counter,' he said. 'Come over here.'

She shifted her weight from foot to foot, grimaced, then wrapped her left arm around her waist and followed him. She leaned against the mahogany and glass counter while he shuffled the mouse to wake up the computer screen.

A prickle of sweat began at the nape of his neck, and he resisted the urge to wipe it away under the woman's scrutiny.

'I can't find anything listed here.'

His eyes flickered to hers for a moment. He could sense stress emanating from every pore as she clenched her jaw.

Her right hand gripped the edge of the counter, her knuckles white.

'Look again,' she urged. 'Please. I don't have much time.'

'One moment,' he said, his heart racing. 'I think I might have something out the back. The 1915 edition, was it?'

She nodded.

Nathan scurried behind a thick brocade curtain separating the bookshop from a small windowless room that served as a cluttered office, crossed the space in three strides and with fingers that slipped on the dial at the first attempt, flipped the combination lock on the safe.

He ran his hand over the book while his heart tried to punch its way out between his ribs. Mid-blue cloth, a darker blue embossed title, and the author's name underneath in tiny lettering almost as an afterthought, it felt heavy in his grip despite its size.

He closed the safe and went back to the counter.

'Here it is.'

A palpable relief washed over the woman's features as she reached out for it.

'Thank you, I can't tell you how grateful I am—'

A shadow fell over her right shoulder and the woman's eyes opened wide at a smooth *click*.

She raised shaking hands.

Nathan held his breath.

Standing behind her, jaw set, eyes blazing under a choppy fringe of dark brown hair, was another woman.

One whose demeanour was the exact opposite of the book-seeking client.

Nathan dropped the book to the counter and glared at the figure before clearing his throat. 'Eva, that's no way to treat the customers.'

'She's not a customer. Not if she's asking for that book.'

'It could be a coincidence.'

'She's bleeding.'

'What?'

Nathan leaned over the counter as the woman removed her left hand from her waist and peeled back her coat.

Sure enough, a rich blood stain bloomed across her shirt above her hip and now dripped upon the parquet floor.

Eva Delacourt moved until the woman could see her face, and pressed the barrel of the gun to her temple. 'Who are you?'

A single tear rolled over the woman's cheek.

'Flight Lieutenant Kelly O'Hara. I've been shot.'

CHAPTER THREE

Eva lowered the gun, paranoia turning to intrigue.

'How did you know about the book?' she said, her eyes narrowing.

'A friend told me. She said if I came here and asked for that exact book, it was some sort of code and that I'd get help.'

Eva caught the look that crossed Nathan's face, and tried to ignore her heart rate increasing.

Since her last mission, she had been keeping her distance from the covert British intelligence agency that had dictated her life for over a decade. The Section wanted her back – she was one of their best assassins – but she had refused, telling them she needed more time.

After all, it wasn't every day one of their operatives cheated death and made sure an international terrorist's plans to kill millions of people went up in smoke.

Literally.

Despite her reluctance to return to the fold, Eva had recognised the need for a support network amongst her ilk. If it hadn't been for her wiles and network of underground contacts, her last mission would have failed with catastrophic consequences.

Eva ran her gaze over the stricken woman and sighed.

Either Kelly was telling the truth and needed their help, or this was going to turn out to be one of the biggest mistakes of her life.

'Come with me,' she said, tucking the gun into the waistband of her jeans. 'Nathan – shut the shop. Use the family emergency sign.'

'Right.'

She helped the woman around the counter while he hurried out into the rain, collected the sandwich board and then shut the front door and pulled a blind over the glass panel in the middle of it.

After placing a handwritten sign in one of the windows, he jogged to the back of the store, brushed past her and moved ahead of them, clearing a pile of books and discarded newspapers from a tattered armchair before spreading an old blanket across the cushions and helping Kelly to sit.

'What happened to you?' he said.

The woman cried out, grimacing from the movement.

'We were duped – fooled into thinking we were on a secret mission,' she said, her voice weak now. 'I had no idea. I would never have got them into this otherwise. It's all my fault…'

Eva was only half listening, reaching up into a cupboard and pulling out a fishing tackle box. Kelly looked horrified as she turned. 'Don't panic – it's the most practical thing to use as an emergency first aid kit.'

Dropping to her knees, she flicked back the chrome levers and began handing gauze bandages and antiseptic swabs to Nathan.

He pushed his glasses up his nose and gestured to Kelly, colouring slightly. 'I'll need you to unbutton your shirt – is that okay?'

The woman nodded, swore as she shrugged her way out of her light coat, and then removed her shirt exposing a bloody wound above her right hip.

'Shit.' The words passed Eva's lips before she could stop them, and she hitched her hair behind her ears. 'Kelly, can you lean forward a moment? It looks like it was a small calibre weapon but I need to see if it's a through-and-through.'

Kelly gasped and clutched her side, then peered over her shoulder as Eva frowned. 'Did it?'

'No.'

'Then like you said, shit.' The woman sounded exhausted, as if the effort to talk was now too much to bear.

'Who did this to you?' said Nathan.

'I presume they worked for the man who got us into this in the first place.'

'Who was that?'

'He called himself Colonel Paul Richards,' said Kelly. 'None of us had ever seen him before. First we knew about it was back in Lincoln – the three of us were out for a curry when a warrant officer came through the door of the restaurant and told us we were required to report back on duty and that a car was waiting outside.' A sad smile crossed her features. 'Josh was pissed off he hadn't even managed to have a sip of beer before we were interrupted.'

'What happened?' said Eva. She frowned as she worked, cleaning the entry wound as best she could but every time she swabbed away the blood, more bubbled from the hole in Kelly's side.

'We were taken to a small airfield – not our usual base. Colonel Richards was in the car – he said an emergency situation had occurred, and we were the only ones available. He said we would be flown to a NATO base in Eastern Europe where he'd explain more and provide us with our mission details.' Kelly pursed her lips. 'It probably sounds strange to you, but it's not the first time we've been asked to drop everything and run because someone's in the shit. None of us questioned him, and because we knew we'd be running a twelve-hour shift once the mission started, we just got our heads down and slept on the way there.'

'What is it you do?' said Nathan. 'I mean, I take it from your rank that you're a pilot, but—'

'I fly drones. An MQ-9A Reaper.'

Eva's hand froze above Kelly's hip. 'You don't fly those on your own. How many were in your crew?'

'There were three of us.' A tear rolled over Kelly's cheek. 'They shot Josh. At the base. Marie – she's the intelligence officer – suspected something. She said she saw something, before the target was hit by the missile. She said it wasn't a terrorist in the vehicle. She said she knew the man we killed…'

Nathan walked across to a counter beside the door and plucked some paper tissues from a box before returning to the pilot. 'Here.'

'Who did your intelligence officer see in the vehicle?' said Eva. She frowned, bit her lip, then pulled a bottle of iodine from the tackle box and recalled the last time she had treated a bullet wound.

It hadn't gone well.

'Jeffrey Dukes.' Kelly shifted in the armchair and stifled a cry. 'Marie said he's – was – a special adviser to the Foreign Secretary.'

Nathan emitted a strangled gasp that mirrored the shocked punch to Eva's chest.

'Which country was he in?'

The pilot paused.

'Kelly – this is no time for the Official Secrets Act,' she said. 'If you want our help, you need to tell us everything.'

'Okay.' The woman took a deep breath, and blinked. 'Syria.'

'Syria? Why?' said Nathan.

'How the hell do I know?' Kelly snapped. 'I was just following orders. Same as every time I fly.'

'Then what happened?' Eva turned to Nathan. 'Can you get me some water? These swabs aren't working. Towels or something, too.'

'Marie told us we had to leave.' The pilot shook her head, her eyes seeking the curtain between the room and the bookshop beyond. 'I think Josh and I were starting to wonder about the whole thing by then, to be honest. I mean, the airfield was in the middle of nowhere, and looked run down. I don't think anything had flown out of there in years. Marie started to lead us away from the building where the ops centre had been set up – she said we should head for the woods we could see surrounding the airfield and try to make our way out of there.' She sniffed. 'We'd stopped, arguing about whether it was the right thing to do, when... when Josh was shot. One minute he was talking to Marie, next thing I knew, he was dead.'

'Christ.' Eva sat back on her heels and gave the woman a moment to compose herself, her thoughts spinning.

What the hell were they getting into?

'Here.'

She looked up at Nathan's voice to see him standing with a glass jug of water and some clean tea towels.

'That's all we've got upstairs.'

'It'll have to do. Hang in there, Kelly – I'm still trying to stem the bleeding.'

The pilot gritted her teeth while Eva set to work putting pressure on the wound and packing it with soft bandages, then took a deep breath. 'Needless to say, we figured out we weren't on a NATO base. Turns out we were in the south of Belarus.

'What about the command centre you were working in?'

'It was only one of those Portacabin things. They can be transported anywhere on the back of a truck.'

'How did you get here?' said Nathan.

'We managed to get away – Marie said we should split up, that we'd stand a better chance of survival if we did, and that we had to tell someone what happened. It was she who told me the code phrase and where to come. I managed to get a lift with a local. His daughter was away at university in Copenhagen, so he gave me these clothes to wear.'

'Who shot you?' said Eva.

Kelly sniffed. 'I was doing fine until I got to Prague this morning. I hitchhiked through Slovenia and then got a bus over the border. It was stupid – I had my passport on me and used it—'

'So whoever Colonel Richards really is, he had the means to trace you.'

'Yes. I guess so. I was in the market over on Havelská looking for something to eat before coming here when I – I don't know – I could feel someone watching me. I ran down an alleyway, but they got a couple of shots off before I could escape.'

'Didn't anyone hear?'

'No.' Kelly groaned, then scrunched her eyes closed. 'They must've been using suppressors, and there was music playing in the market. I thought I'd only been winged at first – I managed to stumble away and got on a bus full of tourists that was pulling away. It wasn't until it was on the move that I realised this was more serious…'

'Adrenalin will do that to you,' said Eva, her head bowed while she worked. 'Did you come straight here?'

'I saw a road sign the bus passed – a street name I recognised – so I got off at the next stop and slowly doubled back here.' She lifted her chin and met Eva's steady gaze. 'I was careful. I didn't see anyone following me.'

'What about your intelligence officer?' said Eva. 'What's her full name?'

'Marie Weston.'

Nathan paled. 'Where is she?'

'I don't know,' said Kelly, opening her eyes. 'The last time I saw her was on that hillside in Belarus. She was supposed to come here too.'

He turned to Eva. 'I need a word – now.'

'In a minute.' She shook her head to silence him, despite his stricken eyes, then put her hand on the pilot's shoulder. 'She hasn't been here. It's been quiet all morning, and we were closed yesterday.'

'She didn't make it, did she?' said Kelly. 'I'm the only one left.'

CHAPTER FOUR

Eva entered the six-digit PIN code for the electronic door lock to the upstairs flat, ignoring Nathan's shout from the foot of the stairs.

She hurried through the living room and along a short corridor to a bedroom at the back of the building, dropping to a crouch next to a built-in wardrobe, opened the door and peered inside. Pushing her hair from her eyes, she lifted a section of one of the floorboards out of the way and reached into a cavity.

Her skin touched cold metal, and wrapping her fingers around the surface she pulled out first a 9mm pistol and then a compact revolver. Placing them on the floor beside her, she shoved her hand back into the cavity and extracted a box of ammunition.

That done, she replaced the floorboard, closed the

wardrobe door and picked up the weapons before returning to the living room.

Lowering the two guns and the ammunition onto a small wooden table beside an overstuffed leather sofa, she sank into the cushions with a groan.

'Talk about bad timing,' she said under her breath.

She blamed herself – she knew the bookstore was a risk but it had been a convenient place to gather her thoughts after her last mission, a place to recover, and a place of sanctuary during that time.

It had once been her grandmother's shop, until Eva had transferred the title to Nathan as a gesture of thanks before disappearing again – the man had saved her life, despite his lack of training and field experience.

She had found it too difficult to settle, choosing instead to wander through Europe while she tried to work out how the hell she was going to sever her ties with the Section and her past – and whatever the future held if she didn't manage to do both.

There were plenty of people who wanted her dead, and she had only returned to Prague in recent weeks with a reluctance borne from a growing realisation that she wouldn't escape her past without a fight.

And now, this.

'We need to get out of here,' she said as Nathan appeared.

'We can't leave Prague yet,' said Nathan, his eyes wide. 'We have to find the intelligence officer before they try to kill her, too. She'll be trying to make her way to us as well—'

'She'll have to take her chances. We've got to get Kelly to safety while we still can, and we've got to work out what the hell we're going to do with what she's told us. If she's telling the truth, then someone in the British government has got some explaining to do.'

'Eva, please. Twenty-four hours – that's all I'm asking.' Nathan gestured to the window. 'We can keep a lookout for any trouble. You've got weapons here, we know the area, we can—'

'If we stay here, we could all end up dead.' Eva crossed her arms. 'Why are you so concerned about the intel operator? We need to go – before they kill us next.'

Nathan dropped into an armchair facing her, his face ashen.

'Because she's my sister.'

'Your sister?'

Eva froze as Nathan slumped in his chair. 'Are… are you sure? You haven't spoken to her in what…'

'Three years. Not since we've been in hiding.'

'Then how can you be sure it's her that Kelly's talking about?'

He raised his head, misery in his eyes. 'It has to be. She uses our mother's maiden name – and the last time I had contact with Marie, she mentioned she was doing aerial reconnaissance work. She couldn't say what though.'

Eva closed her eyes. 'Shit.'

'What happened, Eva? How the hell did she get mixed up in this?' he said, an urgency in his voice. 'What the hell's going on?'

'We'll find out,' she said, trying to shake off the tired reluctance sweeping over her as she realised her plans for a different life were slipping through her fingers. 'But we have to deal with Kelly first.'

'It's too dangerous to move her,' he replied. He crossed to a table beside a window covered with a net curtain and opened a laptop computer before entering a convoluted password.

When the screen came to life, Eva could see six black and white video images of the front street and side alleyway outside, along with two images of the inside of the bookstore.

'Can you see anyone?'

'No.'

'Then let's move her before they find out she's here. If they can trace her to Prague, it won't take them long.'

'We can't,' said Nathan. 'She's lost too much blood already, and she's weak. If we move her, it could kill her. We have to stabilise her first.'

'Well, we have to get her help – I can't stop the bleeding, and I couldn't see the bullet in the wound either.' Eva exhaled. 'Christ, this changes everything doesn't it? All right. There's only one thing for it.' Eva leaned over and picked up a mobile phone, typed in an encryption code, then pressed the speed dial. 'Doctor Novotný? I need your help. No – we're okay, thanks. We have an unexpected guest... You'll need to park your car a few streets away and then walk. We may be under surveillance... Thank you.'

'He didn't ask what it was about?' said Nathan over his shoulder as she ended the call.

'He knows better than to do that. Even if my phone's encrypted, he's still on an open line. He's only five minutes away – he's just dropped his wife at her mother's house and he'll be straight here.'

The Czech doctor was a friend of a close friend, someone who could be trusted – and someone who had once saved Nathan's life.

She could only hope that he would be able to help Kelly.

Eva rose from the sofa, walked over to the small kitchenette that took up one side of the room and began to pull bottles of painkillers from a cupboard above the sink. 'Why use an RAF crew to pilot a drone on a rogue mission? Come to that – where the hell did this Colonel Richards get his hands on a Reaper?'

'That's what I'm trying to find out,' Nathan muttered, his fingers tapping frantically at his laptop. 'There's no chatter about one being stolen, and all the ones I'm aware of are accounted for.'

'Did Kelly give you a serial number before you came up here?'

'She said there wasn't one on it. It's rare for them to be marked anyway, in case they crash…. Hang on a minute.' He pushed back his chair, and waggled his forefinger. 'Maybe that's it.'

'What?'

'What if this Colonel – whoever he is – managed to salvage a drone that had been written off?'

'Don't those have to be accounted for?'

He managed a smile. 'Not if whoever lost it is embarrassed – or lost it while they were flying somewhere they shouldn't have been.'

CHAPTER FIVE

'If someone's got control of a Reaper, then they'd do anything to keep it a secret, won't they? Especially if it's been used to murder a British diplomat.'

Eva stalked the cheap linoleum floor, her thoughts in turmoil.

'If we're right and it has been stolen, at least that goes some way to explain why Kelly's co-pilot was shot trying to escape, and why she's being hunted,' said Nathan.

'Do you think she's telling the truth?'

'Yes.'

'You seem certain.'

He didn't answer.

Eva checked her watch, then crossed to the table and picked up the 9mm pistol, handing it to Nathan. 'Take this. We'll ask Novotný to get Kelly stabilised, and then we'll get out of here the minute Marie turns up. If she does…'

'She will.'

'I'll make another phone call to see if Decker might know somewhere we can stay, or—'

Movement on the laptop screen caught her eye. 'Novotný's at the end of the next street. I'll go and intercept him to make sure he isn't being followed. You'd better check on Kelly – we've been up here too long as it is.'

'Eva?'

She shook her head and turned. 'We'll talk about this later.'

'We have to wait for Marie.' Nathan pushed his chair back, the sound of the wooden legs scraping across the tiles ricocheting off the walls. 'We can't leave yet.'

'I know.'

She didn't wait for a response, hoping that the ex-Section analyst would be able to focus on the urgent care required for their uninvited guest, and now ruing the day they had agreed to put in place a sanctuary for others like them.

Others who had nowhere else to run.

Retrieving the gun she'd tucked into her waistband, Eva removed the magazine and checked it before slapping it back into place with the heel of her hand, then tore down the stairs to the ground floor.

She swung around the newel post at the bottom and headed towards a service door, releasing the three bolts holding it in place, then tapping in the security code that Nathan changed on a weekly basis.

Eva peered outside, weapon raised, but saw no-one in the alleyway along the back of the shop. Next door, a Chinese takeaway remained closed, its doors shuttered until Wednesday night while its owners took a well-earned break after a busy weekend's trading.

Industrial-sized bins overflowed with empty food cartons, a greasy stench permeating the air and clinging to the brickwork.

She let the door swing shut behind her with a soft *thud*, then set off along the alleyway, gun at her side.

Her neighbours had never worked out what she did for a living, and she had no wish to alert them now. If there was the remotest possibility that Kelly had managed to locate the bookshop sanctuary without drawing attention to herself, then they might stand a chance.

Jogging to the end of the thoroughfare, she crept to the corner of the junction with a narrow lane. A few locals passed by, their eyes downturned as they negotiated the slippery cobbles and clutched umbrellas against the swift breeze whipping along the street, the overhanging buildings crowding the pavement and creating a wind tunnel effect.

Satisfied the people she saw posed no threat, Eva

tucked her gun away and hurried over the crossroads, entering a second alleyway that zig-zagged behind boutique clothing shops and cafés, windows steamed up from the hot food and drinks being served inside.

None of the customers sat at the tables inside paid her any attention as she quickened her pace, keen to intercept the doctor before he got any closer to the bookshop.

The path narrowed, her ankle boots scuffing through discarded cigarette packets, food wrappers and takeaway cartons. A pungent smell of rotting vegetation clung to the brick walls, and she turned her attention away from an overflowing heap of flattened cardboard as a fat rat scurried underneath it.

She spotted the end of the alleyway ahead, a glimmer of daylight breaking through the dull gloom—

The screech of brakes reached her, and she froze before flattening her body against a fire exit door, above which a dead neon sign for a backstreet bar hung above the lintel.

A car horn sounded, followed by an indignant shout that turned to loud Czech swearing, and then an engine revved and the vehicle sped away.

Eva swallowed, exhaled, then walked to the end of the alleyway, her heart racing as she hovered beside the doorway to a gift shop bereft of customers.

There were no assailants waiting for her.

Instead, Doctor Novotný stood leaning against a

lamp post, umbrella held aloft in one hand while the other clasped a large canvas bag, a cigarette dangling from his mouth.

He nodded in recognition when she emerged from the shadow of the gift shop and beckoned to him after checking he wasn't being observed by others.

'Thanks for getting here so quickly,' she said, hustling him back into the alleyway, and gesturing to a side street that would take them to the bookshop a different way.

'It is not a problem.' The man moved efficiently, showing none of the signs of his seventy-plus years as he swung the bag over his shoulder and kept an even pace beside her.

His shaggy grey hair was offset by a neatly trimmed beard. Brown eyes swept the crossroads as they hurried over and down another street leading them to the end of the lane where the bookshop was located.

'What do you have?' he said as they passed the front door of the Chinese takeaway.

'Female, shot,' Eva replied. She reached out for his arm and pulled him to a standstill a moment, pausing to check they hadn't been followed. 'The bullet's stuck. I can't help her, and she's lost a lot of blood since she's been with us.'

'When did she turn up?'

'About an hour ago.'

'Do you know her?'

'Never seen her before in my life.' Eva turned back to him. 'The problem is, she knows Nathan's sister. And apparently, she's in trouble too.'

Novotný shook his head, dropped the cigarette to the pavement and crushed it under his shoe before lowering his umbrella.

'There's always trouble where you're involved, Miss Delacourt.'

CHAPTER SIX

Eva knew trying to save Kelly would be hopeless the moment she peered into the room at the back of the shop and saw Nathan's face.

He looked up as she pulled back the curtain to let Novotný go in ahead of her, his features pale as he crouched next to the tattered armchair and held Kelly's hand.

'Her pulse is weak,' he said, moving out of the way as Novotný gave him a gentle shove. 'She was murmuring under her breath for a while, but she's fading…'

Eva didn't hear the rest of what he said.

Kelly cried out in pain, her eyes opening in shock, tears streaming over her cheeks.

Novotný placed his bag next to the chair, pulled on protective gloves and began to examine the damage to the woman's abdomen. His fingers gently traced her skin while he spoke in a calm voice, soothing his patient as he worked.

Eva ran her gaze over the blood-soaked blanket, the tea towels thick with the dark red colour, and knew they were too late. She had seen wounds like this before – and Kelly had expelled copious amounts of energy fleeing the market where she had been shot to get to safety.

If the woman had been treated at the scene, if she had been able to reach a hospital, if—

'Eva.'

Novotný's voice penetrated her jumbled thoughts, and she blinked.

'Yes?'

The doctor had his bag open, a syringe in his hand. 'I'm going to give her a shot of morphine. Kelly – this will help the pain, okay?'

'Wait.' Despite the pain, the drone pilot's voice was firm. 'I need to tell you… the Reaper was carrying four Hellfire missiles. I only used one of them. Whoever's flying it now…'

'Has another three missiles up their sleeve.' Eva exhaled. 'Bloody hell. Do you know where the missiles came from?'

Kelly gave a weak shake of her head. 'They were loaded when we got there. I'm sorry. I don't know anything else.'

'And now, please – let me treat my patient,' said Dr Novotný.

The drone pilot closed her eyes as the needle met the skin of her arm.

Nathan crossed his arms over his chest and turned away, unable or unwilling to meet Eva's eye.

She hovered beside the doctor, nibbled at a ragged thumbnail and then raised an eyebrow as Novotný dropped the used syringe and needle into a plastic box before sealing the lid.

He straightened, then pointed to the door. 'A word?'

Eva tapped Nathan on the arm as she passed him, then waited until he joined her and the doctor on the other side of the curtain. She leaned against the counter and lowered her voice.

'She's not going to make it, is she?'

'I am sorry, but no.' Novotný held up a sealed transparent glass bottle. Inside, a bloody shard of metal rattled across the bottom. 'Do you know what this is?'

'I know it isn't a bullet.' Eva peered closer. 'Is – is that a dart?'

'It is, but not a variety I'm familiar with. It's designed to fragment once it penetrates the skin.' He glanced over his shoulder to where Kelly lay, her eyes closed and her breathing shallow. 'I believe your friend has been poisoned. Whatever substance was used, it was mixed with an anti-coagulant agent to make sure the bleeding will not stop.'

'We'll need to find out what it was,' said Eva. 'I've never come across anything like this before.'

'I will arrange for this to be sent for testing. Discreetly, of course.' The doctor sighed and looped the strap of his canvas bag over his shoulder. 'The poison is attacking her vital organs. Even if she was able to make it to a hospital, I doubt very much they could do any more than I've just done. At least with the morphine, she is no longer in any pain.'

'This complicates things.'

'No shit,' Nathan muttered. 'Now what do we do?'

'Find out who did this to her,' said Novotný, his eyes moving from Nathan to Eva. 'You owe her that much.'

'I was trying to leave all of this behind, Doc.'

'I know.' A sad smile flittered across his face and he reached out for her arm. 'But sometimes in life, we don't get a choice. Besides, your friend is worried about his sister.'

Eva wriggled from his grasp. 'Given what's happened to the rest of her crew, I think he's got every right to be.'

'What about Kelly?' said Nathan.

Novotný bowed his head. 'I do not think she will last long. She will fall into a deep sleep now. I will send someone around to, erm, take care of her later. Will that be all right?'

'Jesus.' Eva placed her hand on the doctor's arm.

'Yes – sorry, Novotný. Please do that – but be careful. We might be compromised. Your man will need to watch out.'

'Do you have a spare key?'

'Here.' Nathan pulled out a keyring and handed over a small brass key. 'You can have mine to the back door. I'm guessing that if we have to leave, we won't be going out the front.'

He swiped his phone screen, his brow puckered. 'Cameras are showing the streets are clear. No-one hanging around. We're still safe – for the moment.'

'You have a lot to do,' said Novotný. 'I will leave via the alleyway, if that is all right with you, Eva?'

'Go back the way I brought you here, but turn right at the crossroads and then cut through the convenience store at the end of the street to get back to your car, just in case.'

'I will.'

'I owe you. Again.'

He waved away her thanks. 'You would help me if I needed it. Besides, Decker vouched for you, and anyone he says is a friend of his, is a friend of mine.'

He slipped through the back door and into the alleyway, setting off at a brisk pace.

Eva watched him go, made sure he reached the end of the alley without incident, and then turned to Nathan.

They stood for a moment, a shocked silence between them, and then he sighed.

'Here we go again.'

She choked out a bitter laugh. 'It wasn't going to last forever, was it?'

'We're going to need help, Eva,' he said. 'We can't do this on our own. Not this time.'

'What are you proposing?'

She could hear the edge in her voice, feel the sudden spike in her heart rate as she waited for his answer.

'Call London. Tell them what's happened.'

Eva sucked in a breath and turned away, crossing her arms over her chest. 'After all this time? How do you think that's going to go down?'

'A lot better than when someone else lies about how Jeffrey Dukes died.'

'Kelly could be lying.'

'And I don't have the means to check her story from here.' Nathan stepped closer. 'Please. I need to know what's going on. I need to know what the hell Marie's got herself into, and I need to know why they were given that mission.'

CHAPTER SEVEN

London, England

Miles Newcombe watched with growing alarm as a representative from the Prime Minister's office paced the room in front of a satellite image displayed on the opposite wall, and ignored the nudge to his elbow from the man on his left.

He was getting a crick in his neck after several hours listening to theories and excuses while self-appointed experts and advisors provided their opinions, each becoming more frantic while new information was issued and disseminated amongst the assembled men around the oval beech-coloured table.

The current speaker was a man in his late twenties, sweat patches under the arms of his Oxford blue shirt while he wore out the carpet tiles with his nervous pacing.

A lingering stench of body odour, burnt coffee granules and panic filled the space as the young man spoke, his message clearly enunciated.

They were all in the shit, and the Prime Minister wanted to know what they were going to do about it before the opposition leader caught wind of the debacle and demanded her immediate resignation – along with theirs.

Heads would roll, that much was certain.

Now it was simply a case of deciding whose – and when.

Miles blinked and loosened his tie, then rolled his neck from side to side before lowering his gaze to a coffee stain on the inside flap of the manila folder he'd been handed upon entering the conference room five hours ago, the current speaker's words doing nothing to alleviate the growing sense of unease emanating from the men around him.

Except for the man who sat to the left of Miles.

Gerald Knox – Section Chief, Cold War veteran and ex-MI6 stalwart emitted a sigh, exquisitely timed to fill the space left behind as the Prime Minister's man paused to take a breath from his monologue.

'That's all very well, Sebastian,' he said, holding up a hand to silence the man from the Home Office seated opposite who had opened his mouth to protest, 'however you fail to understand the complexity of the situation at hand—'

'Not to mention the delicate handling that this matter will require,' interrupted a sandy-haired acolyte from the Ministry of Defence, who shot a glare across the table.

'Handling that *your* department would have done well to partake in several days ago, instead of assuming this was another paper-shuffling exercise.'

Knox's barked retort bounced off the thin walls.

The MoD man's mouth dropped in shock, his face turning red.

Miles fought back the urge to smile, and instead reached forward for a glass of water and took a sip.

He watched as the PM's man – Sebastian Forbes – shrivelled under the scrutiny of his more experienced peers, and wondered if his degree in political science had prepared him for the full wrath of an interrogation by proxy.

Probably not.

After all, it was the Prime Minister who had determined the meeting should be held at short notice and without preparation.

As Knox had said to him before the meeting, this was a face-saving exercise.

The resulting hours were simply to decide whose face wasn't going to get saved this time around.

Miles lowered the water glass and cleared his throat.

'When was the shipment agreed?' he said. 'And, who signed it off without checking it matched the purchase order and the manifest?'

'Now, listen here—' The voice belonged to Edward Toskins, Minister for the Department of International Trade. He leaned forward in his seat at the head of the table and banged his fist on the veneer surface. 'I will not have this outrageous claim undermine the important work we do with regard to foreign trade development.'

Miles reached for the water jug as it wobbled alarmingly, then flicked to another page in the dossier compiled by MI6. Ignoring the shocked glances aimed his way, he held up a manifest obtained by a keen-eyed customs official in İzmir.

'Several items in this arms shipment contravene Her Majesty's Government's own policies and your export watch-lists,' he said. 'Not to mention the fact that the Prime Minister has expressly stipulated in recent press briefings that past mistakes will not be repeated. On top of that, we now have four missing Hellfire missiles that no-one in this room can account for, am I right?'

Sebastian's face showed the first signs of relief since the meeting had started, his shoulders relaxing as he interpreted Miles's intervention as an excuse to scurry back to his seat.

'Those missiles went missing from the shipment after the deal was signed off by this department,' Toskins blustered. 'We had no idea—'

'Therein lies the problem, Edward,' Knox drawled. 'You have no idea.'

A smattering of laughter filled the room as Toskins pushed back his chair.

'I've never been so insulted in my life,' he said. Turning to Sebastian, he gathered up his papers and shoved them into a battered leather briefcase. 'When the PM decides that she wants to have a sensible conversation about how to handle this matter, perhaps you could ask her to afford me the courtesy of a private meeting instead of expecting me to explain matters of departmental interest to her post-graduate lackey and this... this... kangaroo court.'

Miles shook his head as Toskins strode towards the door, wrenched it open and slammed it back in its frame, causing the walls to shake. 'And the general public wonder why it takes so long to sort out government policy.'

'Indeed.' Knox rose to his feet, raised his hands on the table, and took a moment to eyeball the remaining men in the room. 'Despite the Minister's comments that this meeting was convened in order to single him out for embarrassment, the fact is that everyone in this room is responsible for the security of this country, and every single one of us failed to protect the shipment before it reached İzmir. In the circumstances, gentlemen, we expect your full cooperation in our ongoing audit of events as to how those Hellfires went missing.'

Murmured responses accompanied an uncomfortable shuffling of arses in seats at the Section Chief's words – arses that Miles had no doubt Knox would kick from here to the Arctic Circle if they didn't form an orderly queue at his office door with their updated reports by the end of the week.

Knox relaxed, and gestured to Sebastian. 'This would be a good time to adjourn this meeting, Forbes. I do believe the Prime Minister can expect a full and thorough update by close of business Friday.'

'Thank you, Gerald,' said the PM's representative, his voice emboldened by the chief's interference. 'Much appreciated, everyone.'

A rumble of voices filled the room while chairs were pushed back, shoulders were slapped, and a loud braying voice belonging to a middle-aged man from Toskins' department suggested drinks at the sports bar down the road.

'The mobile phone reception's crap,' he said with gleeful enthusiasm to a colleague he grasped by the shirt cuff, 'so no chance of being interrupted. I don't know about you, but I need a bloody drink after that.'

As the room emptied, Miles swigged the last of his water, slipped his papers and laptop into a black canvas backpack propped against his chair, then rose and stretched his back muscles.

Beside him, Knox thumbed through his emails on his phone, then shot him a tight smile.

'That went as well as could be expected, don't you think?'

'You enjoyed every minute of it.' Miles shouldered the backpack and followed the chief to the door. 'I'm not sure Sebastian's going to get a warm welcome back at Number 10 though.'

'He'll live.' Knox elbowed his way past a pair of delegates from MI5 who had sensibly remained silent during the heated discussions, and led the way out into a low-ceilinged corridor underneath Lambeth Palace.

'Sir? Chief?' Knox's secretary beckoned to him, her voice carrying across the throng from where she stood beside the opposite wall. 'It's urgent. Ops room, sir – now.'

'I'll see you shortly.' Knox gave Miles a curt nod, and turned away.

'Actually, he's required as well.' Jenny gave an apologetic shrug. 'They didn't say why, only that you were both needed ASAP.'

'What's going on?' said Knox as they drew closer.

Jenny lowered her voice. 'The code word provided was "Buchan", according to Greg who intercepted the signal.'

A familiar kick in his chest accompanied Miles as he hurried out of the conference room after Knox, accompanied by familiar feeling that was both anticipated – and dreaded.

'We'll reconvene with Sebastian once we have more

information from MI6,' the Section chief was saying under his breath as they passed the lift and turned along a narrow windowless corridor. 'I want to make sure whatever went wrong with that arms shipment doesn't come back to bite us in the backside or present us with new problems. I mean, for goodness sakes – what the hell was Toskins thinking?'

'What about Jonathan Amberley's insistence about delicate handling?' said Miles as they reached a sealed door. 'The MoD might have a point there.'

'We're the Section,' Knox growled, stabbing a finger at a series of buttons set into a security panel in the reinforced concrete wall. 'We don't do delicate.'

CHAPTER EIGHT

A cold spike of adrenalin wound its way through Eva as she watched Nathan monitoring a secure line through his laptop to their old paymasters.

Ever since they had retreated from London, ever since she had barely escaped her last mission with her life, they had severed contact.

She and Nathan had ignored repeated attempts to connect with the Section, cut themselves off from the old drop-off locations and hoped they would be left in peace.

She turned away and peered through the net curtain over the front window, watching as rain droplets ran down the glass, capturing the dull daylight before pooling on the sill. A small group of tourists passed beneath the flat with bright umbrellas raised as they hurried after a tour guide, no doubt eager to find a café within which to shelter.

She sighed, took a step back and lowered the blind designed to shield the flat from prying eyes – and heat sensor equipment.

It was just one of many modifications she and Nathan had made since arriving back in the city, and another way to ensure their privacy and safety.

A single trail had been left open for those in need though, and despite knowing she would do it again if she had to, Eva was beginning to wonder if it had been worth the risk.

If someone could arrange for a rogue Reaper drone to murder a special adviser to the British government, then what were their chances of finding out who, and why – and surviving?

'I sent a request through five minutes ago,' said Nathan, rousing her from her thoughts. 'It'll depend whether he's in a meeting or in the middle of an operation but...'

A loud *ping* sounded.

'That was quick.' Eva uncrossed her arms and dropped into a seat beside Nathan.

'Maybe he's missed us.'

She didn't reply, and instead watched as the encryption programme he had written began to process the connection from London, binary code pouring down the screen like rainfall before it cleared and two familiar faces appeared.

'This had better be good,' Knox said, his eyebrows knitted together.

'What he means is – are you both okay?' said Miles, aiming a glare at the Section chief. 'I presume this isn't a courtesy call given the code word used.'

'Correct, and yes we're okay but we have a dying drone pilot on the premises and information about a potential blue-on-blue strike in the Middle East.'

Despite the seriousness of the situation, Eva took some satisfaction in the shocked expressions on the two men's faces.

Knox held up a hand, then lifted his gaze to someone off-screen and clicked his fingers. 'Greg – clear everyone out of the room who doesn't have level five access. Now.'

Eva heard a scuffling of feet, voices in the background, and then silence.

When the Section chief's attention returned to them, she saw the weariness in his eyes.

'Details?'

She kept the briefing short – Nathan would provide more information offline if the chief wanted it. Her job was to maintain their cover here in Prague and keep an eye on the access points around the bookshop in case they were compromised while a strategy was put in place.

'There's one more issue,' she said in closing. 'Kelly mentioned that her intelligence officer may still be trying to reach us. Marie Weston.'

A flicker of recognition passed Miles's eyes, and he opened his mouth.

'My sister,' said Nathan.

'I thought so.' Miles ran a hand across his face. 'How certain are you that she's on her way to you?'

'She was the one who provided Kelly with the code phrase and details about how to find us,' said Eva. 'Obviously if whoever shot Kelly finds her first, then—'

'Your position is compromised if they get her to talk rather than kill her straight away,' said Knox.

'Exactly.'

'What are your plans?'

'I only have limited access to data from here,' said Nathan.

'That was a choice you made when you decided you both wanted to retire,' said Knox, with more than a hint of sarcasm in his voice. 'And, as far as I'm aware, you've both actively avoided attempts to trace your whereabouts to discuss your future with the Section.'

'Can we have this argument later?' Eva demanded. 'Such as when we find Nathan's sister and work out what the hell is going on? I mean, why would someone use a Reaper drone to murder a special adviser to the Foreign Secretary?'

She saw the look that passed between the two men, and frowned. 'What the hell is going on over there?'

CHAPTER NINE

'We're still trying to ascertain the facts,' said Knox.

'Spoken like a true politician, Chief,' Eva shook her head. 'All right, let's hear it.'

'What we do know is that an arms shipment was intercepted before it arrived in İzmir last week. Four Hellfire missiles were stolen from the cargo during transit. Somehow, the seals on the container from the suppliers in the US were broken and then replaced somewhere along the ship's route. We now have to assume that those missiles were used by the drone piloted by Kelly O'Hara and her crew.'

'Shit,' said Nathan, grimacing.

'Exactly,' said Knox. 'Given what was stolen, we have to also assume someone is gathering armaments for an impending offensive strike. The other problem we have is that we don't know where that offensive strike will take place – there are a number of countries in the region with instability issues that could be potential candidates. Added to that, we have no proof about who was involved in the theft – it's too early in the investigation and everyone involved in legitimate arms sales within the British government is busy trying to work out who to blame and how to cover their own arses.'

'And now we have no witness, either,' said Miles, his face glum. 'That's if your drone pilot is telling the truth about who their target was.'

'It's second-hand information,' said Eva. 'Unless and until Maria can confirm that's who she saw, it's hearsay isn't it?'

Knox's brow puckered. 'If this drone strike happened two days ago, it does make me wonder why no-one from the Foreign Secretary's office or the other security services have commented one of their people has gone missing out in the field. Usually that sort of gossip goes around upstairs like wildfire.'

'It's a remote location,' said Nathan. 'I took a look on a basic satellite image earlier. The road Jeffrey Dukes was travelling on, if our intel is correct, is a single track that winds alongside a mountain pass. It's a rocky desert either side of it, no large townships for a couple of hundred miles… it could be days before word got out that he was missing, especially if he was being careful who he shared his itinerary with.'

'I'll see what we can find out from this end – on the quiet.' Miles loosened his tie and frowned. 'What are your plans, Eva? Are you going to wait and see if Nathan's sister turns up?'

She nodded. 'As long as there are no threats and we see no-one who gives us cause for concern, we'll stay here – forty-eight hours, max. Anything longer than that, and it'll start to get too risky.'

'Agreed. I'll get onto Waddington where the RAF's drone aircraft are based,' said Miles, his brisk tone implying he was already two steps ahead of the rest of them. 'I've seen no intel about a crew going missing, or any security alerts about a missing drone for that matter.'

'Don't hang around waiting to get that sort of information over the phone. Get a car to drive you up to Lincolnshire the minute we're done here,' said Knox. 'Speak to Kelly's commanding officer and ask him if any other crews have been threatened or approached in the past few weeks.'

'Speaking of drones,' said Nathan, 'I wondered – if the drone hadn't gone missing with the crew, then how the hell did the bloke masquerading as a colonel manage to get hold of one? Are you aware of any that have been hacked and stolen?'

'No,' said Knox.

'What about drones that are missing in action – crashed, I mean?'

'We'd have to make enquiries with the Defence Secretary,' said Miles.

Eva could almost hear him squirm. 'Is that going to be a problem?'

Knox grimaced. 'Jonathan Amberley isn't exactly a fan of the Section at present. Probably doesn't like the fact that as Section chief, I get to report directly to the PM. In the meantime, what are you going to do?'

'I'm going to see if I can get Decker to help us.' She ignored the bitter laugh that followed her words. 'We'll be in touch as soon as we've got some more news.'

'Try not to leave it so long next time,' Knox retorted before the screen went blank.

'Does the phrase "a can of worms" spring to mind?' said Nathan, closing the encryption programme and returning the screen display to the series of security cameras.

'All the time. I'm going to check on Kelly.'

Nathan followed her down the narrow staircase after securing the door to the flat, and she swept her gaze over the empty bookshop.

It was habit, that was all, ingrained from years of specialist training and then years out in the field having to survive undetected – both as hunter and hunted.

She would leave nothing to chance.

But nothing moved.

No-one sprang from behind a bookshelf to place a gun against her head.

Situation normal.

Except for a broken woman who lay dying on the premises.

Eva swept back the curtain and peered into the office.

The pilot sat slumped in the armchair, a red stain blotting the fresh dressing Novotný had placed against her abdomen to stem the worst of the bleeding.

Crossing the room, Eva reached out and placed her fingers against Kelly's neck.

Her pulse was weak, faint.

'Eva?'

She straightened at Nathan's voice, and wandered back out to the counter.

His face troubled, he leaned against the till. 'I don't know if I want to do this again.'

'I don't think we have a choice.' She sighed. 'I don't think we've ever had a choice.'

They turned at the sound of a frantic banging on the frame of the front door.

Nathan's eyes widened. 'Do you think they followed her after all?'

Eva retrieved her gun from her waistband, released the safety, and took a deep breath.

'There's only one way to find out.'

CHAPTER TEN

Eva motioned to Nathan to move behind the curtain, and hoped he was carrying the gun she'd given him.

Despite his background as an intelligence officer for the Section and never experiencing in-field action – until he'd met her – he had received training in small firearms when he first joined and she had ensured that his skills remained up to date.

Adequate, at least.

Although he wasn't a natural killer, she knew she would be able to rely on him if it came to that.

She wove between the bookshelves, peering between them as she passed in order to assess the threat.

Beyond the glass panel insert in the front door, between the crack of light showing between the blind that Nathan had pulled down and the frame, she could make out the figure of a slight woman with short brown hair wearing green military overalls.

The woman peered over her shoulder, then turned back to the door and raised her fist once more, her face distraught.

'Shit.'

Eva dashed across the parquet flooring, pulled the key from her pocket and unlocked it, wrenching it open.

'Get in – now. You stand out like a sore thumb dressed like that.'

She pulled the woman over the threshold before slamming the door shut and locking it once more.

Keeping the gun trained on her, she half-dragged the woman towards the rear of the shop, spinning her around beside the counter.

'Name.'

'Marie Weston.'

'Marie?'

Before Eva could stop him, Nathan emerged from behind the curtain, his gun held loosely in shaking hands.

'Marie!'

He placed the gun on the counter and brushed past Eva, enveloping the newcomer in a bear hug.

'Thank God, you're safe,' he muttered. 'I've been worried sick.'

Eva flicked the safety on her own weapon, tucked it into her jeans and sighed. 'I take it this is your sister?'

Nathan shot her a warning glance. 'Marie, this is Eva Delacourt.'

'You're here,' the woman said, between staccato breaths. 'You're actually here. I wasn't sure if it was just a rumour I'd heard. Where's Kelly? Did she make it here?'

Eva pursed her lips and gestured to the back office. 'You'd best come through.'

Fear passed across Marie's face before she squared her shoulders and followed Nathan. She emitted a short, shocked gasp at the sight of Kelly, then dropped to her knees and reached out for her hand.

'She was like this when she got here,' Nathan explained. 'She told us what happened to you. She was shot this morning – she says she was in a market in Havelská when it happened.'

A tear slid down Marie's cheek, and she wiped it away. 'Those bastards. She's dying, isn't she?'

'We had a doctor come to see her – a friend. He couldn't save her, but he did give her some morphine to help with the pain,' said Nathan. 'I'm sorry. It's all he could do.'

Eva leaned against the door frame and let the woman have a few more moments before stepping forward.

'Kelly managed to get a change of clothes.'

Nathan's sister glanced over her shoulder, a sad

smile flickering on her lips. 'She always was more resourceful.'

'It paid off,' said Eva, keeping her tone even. 'No-one followed her to our bookshop, yet they managed to track her to Prague from Belarus.'

Marie's shoulders slumped as the realisation hit. 'Shit. They'll be looking for me too, won't they?'

'Probably.'

Her bottom lip trembled. 'I'm so sorry. I didn't think. I just wanted to get here—'

Eva shook her head, trying to batten down her fury at the woman's naïveté. It wasn't her fault, she reminded herself. She was just like Nathan was when they first met – too used to sitting in front of a computer screen, instead of fighting her battles on the ground.

'First things first – Marie, this is going to sound harsh but you need to say your goodbyes to Kelly. You look about the same build as me, so you can change into something less conspicuous upstairs. Then we'll have to consider our options.'

'While you're doing that, I'll let Knox and Miles know that you've made it here in one piece,' said Nathan. He crossed to the counter and retrieved his gun. 'With any luck, we can keep it that way.'

CHAPTER ELEVEN

Miles raised his gaze from the tablet screen as the government-registered car slowed, and peered through the tinted glass to his left.

Two razor wire fences separated the road from the military installation, one beside the verge and the other ten metres beyond it in a sea of yellow-green grass bearing signs of purposeful neglect.

In the distance, he spotted a figure with a large dog prowling the inner fence line, their pace unhurried. Beyond the patrolling guard were low-slung buildings hunkering in front of two large olive-green hangars, both of which had the doors closed to prevent prying eyes from seeing inside.

The whole landscape emitted a no-nonsense, military atmosphere while a grey sky hung overhead, an almost malevolent tinge to the colours in the clouds.

He shivered at the sense of foreboding creeping across his shoulders, and then glanced down at the screen.

His instructions from Knox were clear, and Miles had no doubt that time was not on their side, evidenced by the way Knox's driver, Harris, had completed the anticipated three-hour journey north in a little over two and a half.

The fence line stopped suddenly, sheared away and broken by an entrance with heavy barriers across it.

Harris eased to a standstill beside a guardhouse and wound down his window before murmuring their names to the man who peered past him and towards his passenger.

Miles reached into the inside pocket of his jacket and extracted his wallet, his thumb brushing against a photograph of a twin boy and girl. He smiled before a pang of guilt seized him.

He hadn't spoken to them for a long time now. The notion of adopting them had been taken out of his hands and passed to a discreet group of people within social services who, having taken one look at what he did for a living, decided that perhaps he and his wife wouldn't be suitable foster parents for the children, and swept them away.

'Sir?'

Glancing up, he saw Harris peering at him in the rear-view mirror, a quizzical expression on his face.

'Sorry. Here you go.'

He handed over his identification and watched as the guard moved back to his brick and bulletproof glass hut, closing the door behind him.

The barriers remained lowered.

Miles peered through the window while the guard spoke into a phone, his eyes never leaving the car while he listened to the response from the other end.

Eventually the man nodded, apparently satisfied they were who they said they were, and that they were expected.

As the door to the guardhouse opened, Harris extended his hand for the IDs and listened while the guard gave instructions about where to go once the barriers were raised, and which areas to avoid.

Miles took a moment to rest his head against the back of the black leather seat and closed his eyes as the electric whirr of the window rising reached him and the car eased forward.

The last few nights had been sleepless, worrying about the breached arms shipment, managing the vast swathes of information his group of intelligence analysts had been required to sift through – and now, this.

'We're here,' said Harris as the car braked to a standstill moments later.

Miles opened his eyes and blinked.

The car had stopped outside one of the low

cinderblock buildings that looked as if it had been built back in the 1950s.

As he pushed open the door, a chill wind buffeted against him and he squinted across the wide concrete expanse to a cluster of other buildings, and wondered how it was that with a contingent of several thousand personnel on site he could only spot half a dozen.

Even those seemed to be in a hurry to get somewhere.

Despite this, beyond his position he could see a cluster of accommodation blocks, social and sports clubs – all the trappings of a major RAF centre of operations. It was hard to counter the view with the knowledge that the base was the home of the UK's Intelligence, Surveillance, Target Acquisition and Reconnaissance group.

If he ignored the hangars casting shadows over his shoulder and the razor wire fence still visible from where he stood, he could almost imagine this place to be a normal mid-sized town, such was its size.

He turned at the sound of a creaking door to see a man in his twenties wearing a navy V-neck jumper over uniform trousers beckoning to him.

'Miles Newcombe?'

'That's me.'

'This way please, sir. Wing Commander Pine is expecting you.'

After signing in without reading the small print on

the form that surely threatened a dark cell should he ever speak of what he heard or saw while on site, Miles followed the man along a short corridor and through a door to his left.

A man stood facing the window, RAF uniform crease-free and his light brown hair cut short.

'Miles Newcombe, sir,' said the younger man, standing to attention.

The man at the window turned, keen blue eyes assessing Miles for a moment before extending his hand. 'Wing Commander Simon Pine.'

'Thanks for seeing me at such short notice,' said Miles, returning the firm handshake.

Pine nodded. 'That'll be all, Smith.'

'Sir.'

The door closed, and Pine gestured to one of the worn vinyl-covered chairs in front of his desk. 'Please, take a seat, Mr Newcombe. What can I help you with? The woman who called was cagey about the subject matter, but said it was a matter of national security.'

The Wing Commander's brusque tone gave way to one of intrigue as Miles took out his tablet computer and scrolled through the file attachments Nathan had sent to him after their conversation.

'We have a situation that's come to light in the past few hours,' he began, 'and we have reason to believe that one of your Reaper crews has been kidnapped and then systematically hunted down after completing a rogue mission over the Middle East.'

Pine's jaw dropped, before he recovered and held out his hand for the tablet. 'I find that incredibly hard to believe, Mr Newcombe. If a crew had been kidnapped, we'd have known about it straight away. We have our own police squadron based here, after all. What evidence do you have?'

'A first-hand witness account from this woman, Flight Lieutenant Kelly O'Hara. Do you recognise this photograph?'

Nathan had taken her photo as she'd drifted into a morphine-fuelled deadly slumber and sent it across while Harris had negotiated the M1 motorway via the overtaking lane, Cambridge flashing past the window in mere moments.

The Wing Commander grimaced as he took in the pale features of the Reaper pilot. 'I don't recognise her, but we have nearly 3,500 personnel on base here.'

'We can also confirm that Kelly has informed us that her sensor operator Josh Connor was shot and killed once their rogue mission was complete.'

Pine's expression changed from shock to horror as Miles described what had taken place two days ago, his hand trembling as he handed back the tablet. He placed his palms on the desk as if to take a moment to calm himself before speaking.

'As I said, if a crew had been forcibly removed, we'd have known about it,' he said.

'What about if that crew wasn't on base at the time, but at a restaurant in Lincoln?' said Miles. 'Does 5 Squadron police the city and all the places around here that off-duty personnel might frequent?'

'Of course not.'

'Then, please – have your people check the records of anyone on leave this week who hasn't reported in, or who hasn't been seen since leaving base.' Miles leaned back in his seat. 'I'll wait here.'

Pine pushed back his chair, rapped the knuckles of his left hand on the desk, then nodded. 'All right, I will. Can I have someone bring you a coffee or anything?'

'I'm fine, thanks.'

The door closed behind the Wing Commander, and Miles exhaled.

He was pacing the carpet fifteen minutes later when Pine returned, his expression perplexed.

'That didn't take long.'

The Wing Commander said nothing, closed the door and leaned against it, his brow furrowed as he tapped a manila folder against his thigh. 'I had one of the administrative staff run their names through our personnel records,' he said. 'None of their names appeared in the search.'

'System error?'

'We discounted that after extending the search to

account for all UK bases and those overseas.' Pine blinked. 'No-one by the name of Kelly O'Hara, Josh Connor or Marie Weston turned up.'

Miles frowned. 'You mean it was a covert operation? That you weren't told what they were doing?'

'No.' Pine strode past him and threw the manila folder on the desk. 'I mean they were never here. Those three crew members were never in the Royal Air Force.'

CHAPTER TWELVE

When Marie walked into the living area of the flat towelling her wet hair, Nathan could see by the slight spring in her step how much more resilient his sister had become.

Some of the exhaustion had evidently ebbed away under the hot jets of the shower, and her appearance was refreshed with a change of clothing – a spare pair of jeans and a sweatshirt of Eva's instead of the green outfit she'd arrived in.

The afternoon had passed quickly while he and Eva pored over satellite images and maps of the area where Marie had said the drone attack happened, while the intelligence coordinator slept on in Nathan's room, oblivious to the hive of activity in the rest of the flat.

He peered at her over the top of his laptop, then

pushed it away and crossed the room, pulling her into a hug. 'I'm so glad you're safe.'

'I'm glad I managed to find you,' she said, her voice unsteady. 'I wasn't sure if it was just one of those rumours that goes around, or whether you were really here.'

'I'm sorry we couldn't save Kelly.'

'The only ones to blame for her death are the bastards who shot her. Did she say whether she recognised any of them from the airfield in Belarus?'

Nathan moved to the kitchen worktop, flipping the switch on a kettle and pulling mugs from a cupboard. 'She didn't, no. I think we were lucky to glean as much information as we did from her before…' He blinked. 'Anyway, we're going to have to start going through personnel records so you can see if you spot anyone you know.'

'Okay.' Marie draped the damp towel over the back of a chair. 'Where's Eva?'

'Out the back. On the phone to Knox or Miles, I expect.' He handed his sister one of the steaming mugs of coffee. 'I'd imagine that headquarters is involved we'll have a lot more information coming our way now so we can find out what's going on.'

'What will happen to Kelly?'

'The doctor who treated her knows someone who can…' He sighed. 'God, sorry this sounds awful – remove her body.'

'Will she be sent back home?' Marie hugged her arms around her stomach. 'I mean, her family will want to know what happened to her, won't they?'

'Novotný has some contacts. They'll look after her until all this is over, and then I expect she can be repatriated.' He placed his mug on the counter and leaned forward to rub her arm. 'Her parents will be able to say goodbye to her properly, don't worry.'

He turned at movement and saw Eva standing outside her old bedroom, her body rigid and silhouetted against the streetlight shining through a small window at the far end of the hallway.

Even though her face was in shadow, he could sense an energy radiating from her, a fierceness that he hadn't seen in months.

The skin on his forearms prickled as she stalked towards them, her jaw clenched as she emerged from the shadows.

'Fresh coffee here,' he said, keeping his tone light. 'Thought you might need some. Figured we're going to be in for a long night.'

'Fine,' she managed.

Marie forced a smile. 'Thanks for the loan of some clothes. I feel better after a shower, too.'

'How did you hear about us?' said Eva, leaning against the worktop beside the sink. 'You never said.'

'In passing.' Marie shook her head. 'I think it was via a British agent who was observing a mission of ours a while back. He waited until everyone else had gone, and then thanked me for a job well done and told me that if I ever needed help, this was where I should come. He was the one that told me about the book you used as a code word, too.'

'The movie was better,' Nathan grinned.

'Sacrilege.' Eva scowled. 'What was his name?

'Sorry?' Marie frowned.

'The man who gave you the address and the code phrase. What was his name?'

'I-I don't remember, to be honest. It was a while ago, and—' she choked out a nervous laugh '—as you'll appreciate, we fly a lot of missions. A lot of people come and go.'

'Would you recognise him again if you saw him?'

'Um, maybe I suppose…'

'Do you always fly with the same crew?'

'Yes.'

Eva choked out a bitter laugh. 'That's all very well, Marie – except there's problem.'

'What?'

'The RAF base commander at Waddington has never heard of you. Or your crew.' Eva pulled out her gun and aimed it at Marie, ignoring the squeak of alarm that Nathan emitted. 'So who the fuck are you really working for?'

Marie raised her hands.

The seconds ticked past, and Nathan took a deep breath, wishing his heart rate would stop rushing blood to his head.

Finally, Marie sighed.

'I'm one of you. I work for the Section.'

CHAPTER THIRTEEN

Eva blinked, her mouth dropping open.

'Give me that.' Nathan pushed back his chair and snatched the gun from her grasp, flicked on the safety and slid the weapon onto the table.

It skidded across the surface, then clanged against the side of his coffee mug and stopped.

'Can you prove it?' said Eva, recovering from her shock.

Marie exhaled and rolled her eyes. 'Seriously? Come on, Eva – I knew where to find you, I knew the code phrase. Hell, I've even heard of the Section. Of course I'm one of you.' She crossed her arms. 'You really think I'd be stupid to turn up unarmed if I was going to try to assassinate you? Have you forgotten that you've still got a reputation in Europe thanks to your last job for the Section?'

'I didn't do it for them.'

'Whatever.'

'Come on, Eva,' said Nathan. 'Enough. I believe her.'

'You would say that – she's your sister.'

'Yes, and I also happen to know that she was approached by Special Intelligence Services when we were at university.'

'Did you?' Marie's eyes opened wide.

He shrugged. 'I used to have to vet all the people the Section wanted to approach about employment prospects. The fact you turned down MI6 six months beforehand worked to your advantage.'

'And yet you didn't know she was flying a Section-owned drone,' Eva said.

He snorted. 'I didn't get paid that much. No, anything like that was passed up to another level. You forget I was only a mortal analyst.'

'I'm still not happy about this.'

'All right, all right.' Marie turned away, walked a few paces and then stopped and peered over her shoulder at them. 'You want evidence, I'll give it to you. I know about the laboratory that got destroyed in Poland. Three years ago, wasn't it? Just before Nathan called me to say he had to go away for a while.'

Eva's mouth went dry. 'How do you—'

'Because we were the ones piloting the drone that blew the laboratory into the next century.'

Nathan raised his hands in the air. 'She scores, she wins.'

'Enough,' Eva snapped, her attention catching his computer screen before she glared at Marie. 'You try anything, anything at all that threatens me or Nathan, I *will* kill you.'

'Understood.'

'Eva?' Nathan stared at her wide-eyed. 'Calm down, all right? I realise this is a shock – it is to me, too – but come on. Give her a chance. At least let Knox corroborate her story.'

'It'll have to wait.'

'Why?'

Eva pointed to his laptop screen. 'Look at the camera feed. There's a car two blocks away, with four men inside. We need to clean out the flat and move.'

'Jesus.' He crossed to the table, moused through the images, and then straightened. 'What about all this kit?'

'Split it up. We'll carry what we can between us. Weapons are a priority, ammunition too.'

'I need my laptop – and the encryption stuff.'

'Fine, but no more than you can get away with, all right? We can source replacements once we find somewhere to get our heads down.'

'Okay.'

Eva was already opening cupboards under the sink, pulling out wet wipes and other paraphernalia. She picked up a spray bottle then sprinted to the first of the two bedrooms and aimed the trigger at every surface, a thick stench of bleach causing her to cough and cover her mouth and nose with her arm as she worked.

It wasn't perfect, but the oxygen-producing liquid worked better than any detergent-based bleach, and would slow down anyone trying to trace their fingerprints.

Eva had used the flat sparingly in the past few months, and Nathan accepted the rules she set in place without hesitation. Every surface was wiped down daily, and their possessions were sparse so as not to draw attention to who they really were.

He knew better than most what her history could conjure, and so even the wardrobes contained little by way of clothing.

They had lived a frugal existence, always ready for the possibility that they would have to run one day.

She dropped the empty bottle onto the bed, then gathered the meagre clothing they kept on hand and marched back to the kitchen. Turning the dial on the oven, she shoved the bundle inside, slammed shut the door and twisted the heat setting up to maximum.

Marie watched with her eyes wide open. 'Do you do this every time you think you're being watched?'

'God, no.' Eva stood with her hands on her hips, appraising the bare flat and calculating what else she could do in the time left. 'But this is more than being watched. No-one sends a car with four men inside to watch. They're a hit squad, no doubt about it.'

'I'm sorry. We shouldn't have come here.' Marie closed her eyes. 'I didn't know where else to go... I don't know who else to trust.'

'It's not your fault. If you hadn't turned up, someone else would've done at some point.' Nathan forced a smile. 'It's why we set up the code word.'

Marie opened her mouth to speak, but Eva held up her hand.

'Save it for later. We're getting out of here now. Nathan – which mobile phone are you keeping?'

'This one.' He held it up. 'It's got the most up-to-date encryption software on it, and...'

'Marie, are you carrying a phone?'

'No – they took them from us before flying us out to Belarus.'

'Fine.' Eva swept up the other two phones from the table, fished hers from her jeans pocket and strode over to the microwave. 'Bring that spare laptop over here as well.'

'You're not going to microwave all of that, are you?' said Marie, her voice incredulous.

In response, Eva pressed the buttons on the front of the microwave, set the heat temperature to the highest point, and stepped back as the machine whirred to life.

Eva pulled across a chair to the centre of the kitchen,

climbed onto it and then removed a nine volt battery from the smoke detector.

Within moments, sparks shot against the heat-proof glass door before flames shot out from the melting phones and laptop and a stench of melting plastic filled the kitchen.

Seconds later, the equipment exploded with a short, sharp bang.

A cheerful *ping* echoed off the kitchen cabinets while the innards of the microwave sizzled and smoked.

'You never did like cooking, did you?' said Nathan.

CHAPTER FOURTEEN

'We've got a problem, sir.'

Miles's attention jerked away from the report in his hand, his other clutching the third cup of coffee he'd wrested from the vending machine since returning from Waddington two hours ago. 'What?'

'Message received on a closed channel from Nathan Crowe,' said Greg, the analyst's eyes never leaving his screen. 'Their safe house has been compromised. Marie Weston was followed. Four men in pursuit in a car registered to a local hire company. I've already run the plates – they were stolen.'

'Shit.' Miles threw the sheaf of paper onto the nearest desk, swigged the last of the coffee, grimaced at the burnt aftertaste and then moved to where the team of three analysts sat facing identical computer screens. 'Where are they headed?'

'He only had time to tell us the street name before they made a run for it – we've got movement in the city centre. I set up facial recognition software on the CCTV cameras around Platnérská and Kaprova streets to get us started.'

'Bring it up on the main display. Everyone – pay attention.'

The large wall-to-wall display opposite flickered to life, twelve panels that together created one huge screen.

'Satellite feed, Emily. Now.'

'Onto it, sir,' replied a young voice to his left.

The analyst toggled the controls and the satellite angle zoomed in from several thousand metres down to a point where they were hovering over the cobble-lined streets of Prague, the manoeuvre completed in under four seconds.

'Where is she, Greg?' he barked.

'Coordinates being entered now.'

'Did Crowe say where they're headed?'

'Negative, sir. He said they're just trying to stay alive at the moment.'

'Jason?' Miles spun around to face the analyst next to Emily. 'I need you to go through all known safe houses on our list. The dark list – not the one we share with MI6. I don't need to tell you all that at the present time, we don't know who our enemy is, where the threat is coming from, or who we can trust. Understood?'

A murmur of responses came back in reply but he

was already moving to the command desk at the back of the secure room, pushing paperwork aside and cursing under his breath.

Eva was on the run with two other targets who were untrained and certainly inexperienced in escape and evade tactics.

And who the hell was going after them?'

'Any sign of their pursuers?' he said, looking up at the large display. 'Anyone keeping an eye on the wider routes around those streets?'

'Establishing that now, sir.'

He bit back a retort, knowing Greg was experienced enough to have already thought of that himself, but unable to prevent the adrenalin surge coursing through his veins.

This was the worst part of what he did in his role as a Section manager – being so far away that he couldn't react, couldn't help, couldn't—

'I've got the hit team.' Emily's voice cut through his thoughts. 'Bringing up a screen capture now.'

A second display overlaid the main image, and Miles saw a beige-coloured four-door car race along a narrow road beside the river before disappearing from sight.

'Where the fuck did they go?' He cleared the space between the desk and the display in seconds, peering up at the images, his eyes searching frantically for the vehicle.

'Under a bridge,' said Emily. 'Here we go – I've got two men on foot now.'

'Get their faces in the system.'

'Sir.'

'Shit.' Miles scratched his jaw as he watched the two figures run up a flight of stone steps leading from the river's edge to the street above. 'Wait – Nathan reported four people in the car. Where are the other two?'

'Still under the bridge with the vehicle, I think,' said Greg. 'They must've split up because it's too hard to get a car around those streets in a hurry.'

'Jason – how are you doing with that list of locations?'

'Working on it.'

'Work faster. We need to send Eva somewhere to keep their heads down until we can get them out of the city.' Miles turned to Greg. 'Have we got any other assets on the ground to assist?'

'Negative, sir.'

'Christ. What weaponry has Eva got? Does anyone know?'

Silence.

'What about vehicles? Have we got any vehicles in the city they could use?'

'Only a motorbike,' said Emily. 'No good with three of them.'

'We've got reports of gunshots near the river,' said

Greg, pressing his finger to his earpiece. 'Two shots fired – a phone call just went through to Prague police.'

'Can you find Eva and Nathan anywhere?' said Miles, unable to keep the urgency from his voice. 'Where the hell are they?'

CHAPTER FIFTEEN

Eva jerked her head back as shards of brickwork exploded a few metres from where she stood, and closed her eyes for a moment.

Only a moment.

A split second later, she shoved Nathan's shoulder. 'Go, go!'

She swung out from her position behind a concrete pillar, fired two shots in quick succession and then peered over her shoulder.

Two silhouettes raced away from her along the river, both Nathan and Marie keeping away from the water's edge and hugging the brickwork archway of the bridge as they ran to lessen the chances of being killed.

Eva turned her attention back to the beige-coloured car now parked at a skewed angle.

Although they had plenty of firepower, the two men sheltering behind it were amateurs.

The taller of the two peered over the roof at her, taking too long to line up his next shot, and she fired before he had a chance to know what had happened.

The bullet pierced the window nearest to her, travelled through the vehicle's upholstery and out the other side.

The man's chest exploded as the force of the shot sent him backwards, disappearing from view.

She gritted her teeth as sirens wailed, coming closer.

'Fuck.'

Three years of solitude, gone.

Now she was fighting for her life against an unknown enemy, and responsible for two people who had very little experience in how to survive being hunted.

Swiping the empty magazine from the gun, she pulled a replacement from her back pocket, slammed it into place, then aimed at the second figure that emerged from behind the car's bonnet.

She fired twice, the echo of the shots thunderous within the confines of the bridge's deep arch, then threw herself behind a stone pillar as the man returned fire.

A pause.

He was out of ammunition.

In a split second, Eva was running.

Towards the car.

Crouching, she waited until she was only a few metres away before she started to squeeze the trigger. Any sooner, and the bullets would have been embedded in the engine block, and not her intended target.

She heard a cry, the sound of a body hitting the pavement.

Sliding to a standstill, Eva edged around the back of the vehicle, weapon ready.

There was no need.

The second man lay slumped across the body of his compatriot, part of his face missing where a chunk of metalwork had pierced his jaw before embedding itself in his brain.

Eva checked her weapon, then blinked as blue lights flashed from the street above the river walk before two Czech police cars tore down the concrete ramp towards her.

'Shit.'

She turned and ran, long strides driving her along the river embankment, away from the car and up a landscaped slope on the other side.

Nathan was waiting at the top beside his sister, his face pale.

'I thought you were gone,' he managed as she drew closer.

She didn't stop. Instead, she tugged at his sleeve and ignored Marie's shocked expression.

'Keep up,' she yelled. 'We're not out of danger yet.'

CHAPTER SIXTEEN

Miles paced the floor, the only sounds in the room that of the air conditioning and the frantic scrabble of fingertips on keyboards.

The sour stench of body odour filled the enclosed space as he reached the far wall and turned back, his gaze falling to the large screen as new information blinked onto the display and CCTV camera angles flashed back and forth.

'Delacourt just broke cover from a side street.' It was Jason this time. 'That's Crowe and his sister behind her. I think I've got somewhere they can go short-term, too. East of their current position.'

'Greg, get hold of Nathan and patch him through to Jason. Talk him through the plan,' said Miles.

Seconds later, Nathan's voice came over the speakers in the room.

The man was out of breath, and Miles wondered how much longer the three fugitives could keep ahead of their pursuers.

'Nathan, we've got a place for you to hide. What's happening there?' he said.

'Two hostiles down,' came the breathless response. 'We're all okay. Eva's just doubled back on our route to see if she can take out the others.'

'The police are at the bridge, and more are on their way,' said Greg. 'Can she do it without drawing attention to your current position?'

'I don't think that's her priority at the moment. Hang on.'

Miles held up his hand for silence while he watched the two figures on the screen duck into a doorway.

Moments later, the two men in pursuit appeared at the corner beside a boutique hotel and slowed to a hurried walk.

'Christ, they don't stand a chance,' said Miles.

No-one answered.

All three analysts were turned towards the screen, their faces stricken.

Helpless, Miles glanced at the other screens while the Czech police vehicles crawled ever closer to the street where Nathan and Marie were attempting to hide.

He had no doubt that the two pursuers would fade away if the police showed up, and that if Nathan and

Marie were taken into custody there would be no guarantee of their safety there, either.

Then, from the shadows of an alleyway opposite, a figure swept into the narrow lane.

Miles held his breath as the woman brushed past the first man, then paused behind the second as if waiting to enter the shop he loitered outside, and moved on.

'Wait. Was – was that her?' said Emily.

The woman carried on, then stopped at the doorway where Nathan and Marie sheltered.

'Miles? You there?'

He watched as the two men staggered backwards and helped each other across the street before collapsing at the entrance to the alleyway, and shook his head in disbelief.

'I'm here,' he managed.

'Eva confirms all four hostiles are down. So, where do you want us to go?'

'Smíchov,' said Jason. 'Take the next alleyway to your right and move as fast as you can. You'll avoid the incoming police vehicles that way.'

'Will do.'

Miles exhaled, then turned to Greg.

'Well, at least we know she's carrying a knife as well as the gun.'

CHAPTER SEVENTEEN

Gerald Knox nodded to the uniformed custodian who greeted him and shrugged off his thick wool overcoat while the man checked his identification.

A second man moved from behind a desk, took his coat from him, politely requested a cursory inspection of the contents of his leather briefcase for security purposes, then handed it back and crossed Knox's name from the register.

'All in order, sir,' said the custodian. 'If you'd like to follow me, the Prime Minister advised that she'll meet with you in the study. Would you care for some tea?'

'Please.' Knox followed him through a maze of corridors and stairways, eventually finding himself on a deserted landing while the custodian rapped on a panelled door before entering.

'Here you go, sir. I'll advise the Prime Minister's staff that you're here.'

'Thank you.'

The man retreated, a soft *click* the only indication he had left the room and shut the door.

Knox paced the Axminster carpet, the soles of his shoes silent on the thick weave as he crossed the room.

Curtains covered the large sash windows of the study while table lamps strategically placed around the space lent a soft glow to the pale yellow walls and cast shadows across the plaster architraves that hugged the ceiling. Bookcases lined the walls containing centuries-old thick tomes on the shelves that were protected by glass doors.

Knox wandered up to a circular hardwood table set for eleven and ran his fingers over the bare surface, recalling the last time he had taken a seat in one of the black leather chairs, then turned before flicking his wrist and checking his watch.

Over twelve hours since Flight Lieutenant Kelly O'Hara had appeared in Prague, dying.

When he reached the end of the room he raised his gaze to the gilt-framed oil painting of a former Prime Minister hanging beside bucolic landscapes, then turned as the door to the left of the marble fireplace opened, and the current incumbent entered.

'Prime Minister,' he said, shaking hands with her.

Grey had peppered her blonde hair over the past twelve months but the creases around her eyes were those of laughter, not the frown lines many of her ministers wore.

The fifty-nine-year-old politician was adept at delegating, managing and leading a country that was now on its own in Europe – and didn't mince her words if her authority was questioned. However, she was known to be fair, a good listener and a brilliant tactician.

Knox hoped he had caught her on a good day.

The woman crossed to one of two check-clothed armchairs set beside an occasional table and waved him to the other. 'This had better be good, Gerald. I've just had to apologise to the President of the United States for cutting short our phone call.'

Knox eased into his seat, and remained quiet.

Sometimes, it was the best option rather than bravely venture an opinion. He'd seen politicians with decades of service wilt under the Prime Minister's sharp tongue.

She waited until a staff member had entered the room and placed a tea tray on the table before retreating, the door closing behind him.

'Right, let's have it then.'

The Section chief opened his briefcase and pulled out a manila folder before taking a deep breath. 'This might take a while, Prime Minister.'

'Right. Well, you talk – I'll pour, shall I?'

When he had finished thirty minutes later, they were onto their second cup.

He remained silent, the ticking clock on the mantelpiece grating on his nerves while the PM ran her gaze over the briefing papers he had handed over.

She wouldn't rush – he wouldn't expect her to in the circumstances – but he had the unnerving sense that she was sizing him up and making him wait.

He cleared his throat. 'Prime Minister, I wondered if now would be a good time to bring in the Minister of Defence on this and perhaps update him with regard to the situation?'

She slapped shut the folder and handed it back to him with a withering glance. 'Out of the question, Gerald. I'm facing re-election in eight months and the less the Cabinet know about this, the better. The last thing I need right now is a leadership contest.'

'As you wish, Prime Minister.' He tucked the folder back into his briefcase and snapped it shut. 'What about funding though, to ensure that my staff can carry out their duties?'

'Gerald, I've spent most of the time since their last escapade smoothing ruffled feathers in Europe, notwithstanding the bioterrorism attack they managed to thwart.'

'I understand that, Prime Minister, but this might be

connected to the İzmir shipment debacle. The Section has the only non-RAF Reaper drone available and it could have been used to monitor the situation in the Middle East if we'd been brought in sooner about that operation. Except now we don't have a crew, because they were kidnapped and coerced into killing the one man who probably had sufficient intelligence to enable us to arrest and charge whoever's behind this. With a rogue Reaper we had no idea existed.' Knox jabbed his finger into the armrest as he spoke. 'That crew were then hunted down and executed. We're lucky one of them was able to escape from all of this unharmed.'

'Does anyone else know that she survived?'

'Only myself, my senior advisor Miles Newcombe and the two ex-Section agents she's currently with.'

'Eva Delacourt and Nathan Crowe?' The PM's lip curled. 'I thought the next time I heard those names we'd have them back here working for us – or under arrest for desertion.'

'This could be our best chance of retaining their services, Prime Minister. After all, it was Eva's idea to create a bolt hole for agents in trouble. If it wasn't for her actions, Marie Weston would be dead too – or worse, traded on the black market for the knowledge she possesses.'

She peered at him over her teacup, then lowered it to the table. 'You'll need to provide more evidence before

I can make a decision, Gerald. I cannot afford another embarrassment.'

'I understand.'

'The crew member who survived…'

'Marie Weston.'

'Yes. I presume Delacourt and Crowe can keep her safe.'

'They'll do their best in the circumstances until we can bring her back here for debriefing.'

'All right. Do what you need to do.'

'I take it then, Prime Minister, I can count on your support to continue the Section's involvement in tracing whoever's behind this atrocity and finding out what is going on?'

'You can, Gerald.' She cleared her throat. 'But let's keep it to ourselves for now, shall we? No need for the likes of MI6 or Jonathan Amberley and his cronies at the MoD to know yet. Not until we know where that drone came from.'

'Of course, Prime Minister.' Knox stood and straightened his jacket before extending his hand. 'I will of course provide you with timely updates as to our progress.'

'I'd expect no less.'

Knox left the room, nodded to the official who closed the door behind him and hurried along the corridor towards the exit.

His phone vibrated in his pocket before he reached

it, and he paused beside an ornate Greek vase to answer it. Knox listened for a moment, then started walking as the caller's words sank in.

'Not over the phone. Meet me at the usual place in a couple of hours.'

CHAPTER EIGHTEEN

Miles pushed the solid brass handrail set into the oak-framed glass door of the exclusive drinking club, the hinges giving way without a sound.

The door swished closed once he'd passed, the late night push and shove of the city outside falling away with some of the stress as he made his way towards the reception desk and shed his overcoat.

A string sonata played through speakers set into the ceiling, and the soft music lulled some of the tattered nerves he'd been nursing since returning from Lincolnshire and then having to observe Eva and the others running for their lives.

The helplessness and frustration was subsiding, but not the worry.

Not after what he had learned from the RAF Wing Commander.

'Good evening, sir,' the concierge gushed, taking his coat with reverence and folding it over one arm.

'Evening. Gerald Knox is expecting me.'

'Very good, sir. He hasn't arrived yet, but requested I direct you to the Deighton bar, through there.'

'Thanks.'

As he passed through an archway to the left of the reception room, Miles inhaled the distinct scent of cigar smoke and money.

Leather wing-backed armchairs in groups of four and pairs were arranged throughout the large space in such a way that the occupants would be shielded from the prying eyes of their neighbours, although to Miles's well-trained ears it seemed that he was the only one present at this late hour.

Beyond the chairs, beyond the walls lined with bookcases and expensive bric-à-brac from all four corners of the world, was a long bar. The brass beer taps were gleaming and the bottles behind the mahogany glistened under strategically-placed spotlights.

A lone bartender looked up from polishing the brass and smiled. 'Evening, sir. What can I get you?'

'A scotch, please.'

'Make that two.'

Miles turned at the gruff voice to see Gerald Knox advancing towards him, the man's face harried as he brushed a lock of hair away from his forehead and shifted his briefcase to his left hand.

'Did your meeting go well, then?'

'As well as could be expected in the circumstances. Actually,' Knox said, his attention turning to the bartender, 'make mine a large, will you?'

The man nodded and moved away, and Miles watched as he selected two crystal tumblers from a collection on a back shelf, checked the glass for stains or chips, and then proceeded to free-pour the drinks.

Miles remained silent until the bartender returned, thanked him and raised an eyebrow at Knox as they took their drinks. 'Where do you want to sit?'

'Over there, at the back near the bookcase.'

He let Knox lead the way, noting that the old spymaster hadn't lost his touch.

The two chairs he had pointed out were away from the curtained windows facing the street, a good distance from the nearest table lamp, and positioned in such a way that between them they could watch both the bartender and the exit.

Good for avoiding both any hidden microphones and over-inquisitive staff members.

As he eased into one of the armchairs, the soft leather enveloping his aching back, Miles glanced at the clock on the opposite wall.

'It's been a while since we had a meeting this late, chief.'

Knox grunted in response, placed his briefcase at his

feet and took a large gulp from his tumbler. 'So, your phone call…'

Miles bit back his frustration, and rested his glass on the arm of the chair, turning it in his fingers. 'When were you going to tell me that you suspected the Reaper crew belonged to us?'

Knox swallowed a second nip, the scotch disappearing at an alarming rate. 'When I was sure.'

'What about the drone that was used? Is that ours as well?'

'No. That's still in its hangar.'

'Where?'

'Switzerland.'

'Switzerland?' Miles clamped his jaw shut after the outburst, sure that his voice had ricocheted off the walls such was his shock. He glanced towards the bartender but the man had his head bowed, evidently used to pretending his clients' voices couldn't reach his position.

'What the hell is it doing there?' he hissed. 'Switzerland is supposed to be neutral.'

'That's why it's there.' Knox shot him a withering look. 'No-one would think to look for it. Not to mention the fact it's centrally positioned so we can send it anywhere within a few hours. It saves on flight time and fuel.'

When Miles raised his glass to his lips, he realised his hands were shaking.

Maybe he should've ordered a double as well.

Knox drained his glass, then held it up and tapped it with his thumbnail and called over to the bar. 'Another two, please.'

'Right away, sir.'

'How are you getting home?' said Miles.

'I'm not. I'm availing myself of one of the guest accommodation suites upstairs tonight. You should, too. Phone your wife. Let her know you're going to be down here for the long haul. We're going to be working some long hours until we get to the bottom of this.'

The Section chief raised his palm for silence as soft footsteps approached the table, and Miles held his tongue while the bartender fussed about setting down a dish of complimentary canapés with their drinks.

When he walked away with Knox's empty glass in hand, Miles leaned forward.

'What did the PM say?'

Thankfully, Knox's drinking had slowed. Instead, his expression became reticent as he cradled the tumbler in his lap.

'We have her go-ahead to support Eva and Nathan in any way we see fit. That includes getting Marie to safety. We also have carte blanche to do whatever it takes to locate the man calling himself Colonel Paul Richards and all persons associated with him. Then we have to find out why Jeffrey Dukes was targeted and murdered.'

'What about the other intelligence agencies?'

Knox shook his head. 'Absolutely not. This is a Section-only investigation. Our crew, our problem. The last thing the PM wants is MI6 or the MoD catching wind of this, so we're going to have to tread very carefully with our questions. She's worried about a Cabinet split and losing her job before the next election if this gets out.'

'Shit. Now I can see why you needed the drink.'

'Indeed. Have you heard from Delacourt this evening?'

'Only within the last hour. They're on the outskirts of the city.'

'Do we know who sent the hit team after them?'

'No names yet, but we have to assume they were reporting to whoever has the rogue drone. They must be the same ones who shot Kelly as well.' Miles sighed. 'Greg hasn't found any trace of them in our system, despite running the images through every database at our disposal.'

Knox shook his head. 'There are more and more mercenaries coming onto the market these days than we can keep up with. What are Delacourt and Crowe's plans for tonight?'

'They're still trying to contact Decker.'

'And we have no idea where he is?'

Miles wrinkled his nose. 'We never did, once he left.

After the last threat was eliminated, he disappeared again. He's like a ghost, you know that.'

'A ghost whose skills would be highly valuable if we could convince him to return.'

'Maybe it's for the best that we don't.' Miles shrugged, took a sip of scotch. 'After all, he helps when Eva asks him. Might be better to leave it that way.'

Knox stifled a yawn, rocking his head from side to side. 'Okay, well I'm sure they'll be in touch once they've worked out where to meet him. In the meantime, I want your analysts working through the intel we got via Kelly O'Hara's version of events as given to Eva and Nathan, and what Marie has told us in relation to the pick-up in Lincoln. That needs to be escalated so we can find out who the driver was that went to the restaurant. Get another pair of analysts to work on the Jeffrey Dukes side of things.'

'Will do, chief.'

'I'll catch up with you at noon tomorrow for a debriefing, but pass on everything you find out to Delacourt in the meantime.' Knox drained his glass and stood, picking up his briefcase. 'I have a feeling she's going to need all the help we can give her on this one.'

CHAPTER NINETEEN

'We can't stay long.'

Eva prised open two slats of the dusty plastic venetian blind and peered out through the window of the cheap motel room to the street below.

Litter cluttered the gutters and a pair of pigeons bobbed between parked cars, flipping over discarded food wrappers and takeaway cartons in their endless search for scraps. In the distance, a siren wailed – a pitiful backdrop to a bleak urban sprawl.

This was the side of Prague the tourists didn't see.

Like any rundown city suburb, it wore its dinginess with reluctance and hunkered at the fringes of the more respectable neighbourhoods.

This was where people came to be forgotten.

Eva let the blind snap back down and turned to

Nathan. 'Do you think you can get hold of Decker on a secure line?'

The analyst wrinkled his nose. 'Depends. It's not like he left a forwarding address before he disappeared, is it?'

She locked eyes with Marie. Sure, she had the woman's word that she was an employee of the Section, and yes she had known where to find them and the code phrase to get help, but…

'We need to make this call in private,' she said. 'Decker won't talk to us if he knows you're here.'

'I can go and stand in the bathroom and run the shower if you don't want me to hear anything,' said the woman. 'I get it. We need help, right? Otherwise, we're all dead.'

'Unfortunately, you're right,' said Nathan. 'Whether we like it or not, until we find out who's trying to hunt you down to stop us finding out what's going on…'

'Don't worry, I'm going.' Marie snatched up a complimentary guide to the city that had been left by the owner on a chipped laminate-covered table. 'I was going to take a look at what there is to do around here anyway.'

Once the bathroom door shut and the sound of the shower could be heard, Nathan beckoned to Eva. 'All right, look. I've got three possible IP addresses for him, two mobile phone numbers and a dark web message room. Which one do I try?'

She crossed her arms over her chest. 'All of them. My money's on the message room though. It's a similar system that he used to use when he was with the Section.'

Watching as Nathan brought up different app windows on the laptop screen and typed in strings of code, she nibbled at a thumbnail and for the nth time since leaving the bookshop wondered what they were getting into.

She needed Decker's company as much as his skills. Nathan was a computer genius, but John Decker would keep her alive – and keep her focused, too. She was no good as a babysitter, having spent years working alone but together...

They might just stand a chance.

'The message room,' said Nathan, snapping his fingers. 'Got him.'

'Really?' Eva stepped forward, unable to keep the surprise from her voice.

'Hang on.' Nathan frowned, scribbled a series of numbers on a scrap of paper, then exited the programme.

'Wait, what are you doing?'

'It's okay, don't panic. He just wants to do this on video. This is another secure contact detail he's using these days, that's all. Just give me a few seconds to connect us.'

The screen flickered across the encrypted connection, then Decker appeared on camera.

'Where the hell is he?' she murmured.

'Tuscany. At his place,' said Nathan out the corner of his mouth.

Eva took in the figure on the screen.

Now in his mid-forties, Decker was sitting at a table in what appeared to be a farmhouse kitchen, wearing a black vest top that exposed sun-browned skin bulging with muscle. His dark brown hair remained cropped close to his skull while days-old stubble covered his jaw. Fierce green eyes peered over a newspaper, a frown creasing his brow.

'What do you want?' he demanded.

'Signal okay?' said Nathan.

'It's fine.'

'The picture's crap,' said Eva.

'It's a cheap-shit disposable phone, what do you expect?'

'Good to see you, too.'

Decker leaned back, keeping the newspaper held upright. He wet his thumb, flicked the page over and lowered his gaze from the phone screen to the text in front of him. 'What do you want?'

'We've got a slight situation here,' said Eva.

'Uh-huh.'

She exhaled, and tapped Nathan on the shoulder. 'You tell him.'

Walking away from the analyst, she paced the threadbare carpet as he spoke and kept one ear on the sound of the shower.

She had no doubt that Marie would have her ear pressed to the bathroom door trying to listen – she would, if she was in the same position – so she reached out and turned on the radio clock plugged into the wall next to the bed. Finding a talk show channel, she turned up the volume before wandering back to where Nathan was concluding his tale of events to date.

'So, that's why we need your help,' said Eva.

'I've got grapes to harvest.'

'Bullshit. They're not ripe yet, it's only May. Besides, you pay people to harvest them for you.'

'I'm busy.'

'You're sat on your arse reading the paper upside down.'

Decker lowered it, glaring at her. 'It's cold there.'

'Don't be ridiculous. We've worked in the Arctic before now, so don't start with the excuses.'

'You have?' Nathan's eyes widened. 'When? Why?'

Eva shook her head. 'It doesn't matter.'

Nathan counted the seconds while the ensuing silence stretched out and Decker's eyes bored into the camera lens. When he opened his mouth, Eva raised her hand to him for silence, her gaze never leaving the man on the screen.

Eventually, Decker spoke. 'Where do you want me?'

'Coming here isn't an option. We already know there are hostiles in the city so we need to make a break for it. Where would you suggest?'

'Remember the place we spent a couple of days after that job in Austria a few years ago while we waiting to see where the Section would send us next?'

Eva narrowed her eyes. 'Is it still there?'

'Abandoned by the CIA four years ago.' Decker winked. 'I changed the locks and set up a camera feed so no-one could get in without me knowing. Do you think you can get yourselves to Germany?'

'I think so. When?'

'I'll give you twenty-four hours. If I don't see you by then, I'm out of there. I'll assume the worst.'

'Understood.'

'Fine.' The older assassin leaned forward, his thumb hovering close to the phone. 'I'll see you then.'

'Decker – wait.'

'What?'

'We'll need weapons, too. One of our conditions to be left alone by the Section was to tone down the armoury.'

'Tone it down? By how much?'

Now it was Eva's turn to look uncomfortable. 'I've got nothing bigger than a couple of 9mm handguns. I'm low on ammunition too.'

'Shit.' Decker snorted. 'All right. I'll see what I can dig up.'

Nathan narrowed his eyes. 'You mean that literally, don't you?'

'Well, I don't grow vegetables in my spare time, do I?' the older assassin snapped. 'Might as well do something useful with the garden.'

CHAPTER TWENTY

Charlotte Hughes took one look at the snag in her fifteen denier stockings and swore under her breath.

She slammed shut the lower drawer of her desk, cursing the rough edge that had caught her leg, then pulled a bottle of clear nail varnish from her handbag and applied a liberal brushstroke to the offending tear.

'I've got a spare pair if you want them,' said a friendly voice.

Peering over her computer screen, she smiled as Simone Barnett hovered by her in-tray with a pile of files in her arms. 'I've got some, but thanks. It's always the expensive ones, too isn't it?'

'I think it's a conspiracy myself.' Simone lowered her voice. 'Heard anything yet?'

'No.' Charlotte bit her lip. 'Maybe his plane got delayed or something. Or he's got no phone signal.'

'That'll be it.'

Voices from the corridor beyond Charlotte's office came closer and Simone forced a smile.

'I'm sure he'll call when he can.'

'Thanks. You're probably right.'

She stifled a sigh as the other woman scurried from her office, and flicked the tab on her computer screen to a list of flights arriving that morning. The one from Ankara had landed a little while ago at half eleven, having made up some time thanks to a tail wind. He hadn't phoned when she'd reached the office at half eight so perhaps he had caught the later one after all.

They had only known each other for a couple of months after an acquaintance had introduced them at a colleague's leaving drinks party in a bar just down the road, but a shared interest in trashy eighties films, theatre performance and rock music had turned into a fledgling relationship that she was keen to nurture.

So far, they'd kept it to themselves though.

Private, and away from office gossip. Only Simone suspected the truth and the only other person who knew for certain was her brother, her closest confidant these past few years.

'How's the report for Toskins coming along, Char?'

Stabbing her forefinger on her mouse, the screen returning to a spreadsheet, she spun her chair around to face Neil Hodges.

'You'll have it in fifteen,' she said, keeping her voice light.

Hodges smiled, exposing uneven teeth. 'Wouldn't like to keep him waiting, would we?'

Charlotte resisted the urge to retort, and turned her back to him.

The man was a self-serving creep who had appeared one day last year having been recruited from a minor department. Since then, he had succeeded in offending every woman in Portcullis House. In his late fifties, a heavy smoker and widowed according to Suzanne, he had somehow managed to charm Toskins within a month of turning up and now here she was, reporting to him.

The problem was, he was good at what he did and administrative support roles at this level were few and far between. Charlotte needed the job – she didn't fancy her chances at finding another role in the City at forty-five.

She blinked back the frustration and set about creating the formulae and formatting that would give Toskins and his team the data they sought.

Hodges' mobile phone trilled and he pushed back his chair as he answered in a braying voice that carried across the small open-plan space they shared with four others, and then proceeded to pace between the desks and chairs as he spoke.

Casting her eye over the last of the sums, she saved the file to the cloud-based secure server and locked her screen before snatching up her mobile phone.

She ignored the look that Hodges shot across the room at her as she weaved behind a colleague's chair and instead kept her attention on her phone screen.

Eleven-fifty.

Surely he would have disembarked by now.

'Morning, sunshine.'

Her head jerked up at the sound of the voice, and she smiled. 'Morning, Laura.'

The woman from the general administration pool was balancing a haphazard pile of padded bags and envelopes in her arms, using her chin to prevent the top-most package from sliding away from her. 'I've got something for you in this lot. Hang on.'

Charlotte followed her over to an alcove housing a series of wire racks above a cupboard used for stationery, and waited while she sorted through the pile. 'How's your daughter getting on at university? Last semester isn't it?'

Laura rolled her eyes. 'Thank God. Costing me a fortune. I mean, she's a good kid but that part-time job of hers doesn't pay enough.'

'Has she made up her mind what she's going to do yet?'

'Travel, apparently. Heading for Australia on a one-year visa.' The woman's eyes grew wistful. 'I just hope she comes back. Ah – here you go.'

Charlotte took the A4-sized envelope from her, then smiled as she recognised the handwriting.

The address had been scrawled in haste – and then she saw the postmark.

Gaziantep?

She frowned, recalling the name of the Turkish town from news reports soon after the Syrian conflict had escalated, its proximity to the border a welcome relief to exhausted refugees.

'Everything all right, duck?'

'It – it's fine, thanks.'

'You've gone quite pale.'

When she looked up, Laura was frowning so she forced a smile.

'Really, I'm fine. Was there anything else for me, or Neil perhaps?'

'No, that's it for today.' Laura winked. 'I'll see you tomorrow.'

'Thanks.'

Charlotte glanced over her shoulder to see Hodges still on the phone. He was standing at the window with his back to the office, barking orders at some other unfortunate soul, and taking no notice of her.

She ran her thumb over the postmark, then tore open the envelope. Pulling out a sheaf of handwritten notes, her eyes fell to the note stuck to the top page.

Be careful who you trust.

'What the hell have you been up to, Jeffrey Dukes?' she whispered.

CHAPTER TWENTY-ONE

Eva's hand shot out to steady Marie as the woman stumbled on the uneven surface, then waved away her mumbled thanks.

The day had grown warm, with bright sunlight dappling through the forest canopy as they wove along a narrow dirt path. The only sounds were their footsteps and a persistent cuckoo's call.

By her reckoning, they had another two hours walking before their next scheduled rest, and she intended to cover as much distance as possible in the time left.

The Czech Republic lay miles behind, the border between it and Germany crossed under cover of darkness before dawn broke.

She had insisted on using buses to get them away from Prague rather than stealing a vehicle and attracting unnecessary attention to themselves, keeping to the quieter local bus routes rather than using the vehicles that swept across Europe, before the small group reached Grafling and started out on foot for the hike to their final destination.

Pulling her sweatshirt over her head and tying it around her waist, she took the bottle of water Nathan held out and took a swig before passing it back.

'How're you doing?'

'Blisters,' he said, and grimaced. 'I thought I'd be all right with all the bloody running I do to keep fit.'

'Different terrain. Will you be all right?'

'Why, are you going to leave me behind if I'm not?'

'Maybe,' she said, and winked. 'But I'd shoot you first to put you out of your misery.'

'That's not funny,' Nathan called as she set off once more.

'What's the name of this place we're heading for?' said Marie, falling into step beside her.

'It's an old CIA listening station.'

'How does your friend know about it?'

'He's freelance.' Eva squinted as they entered a glade, the ground undulating between deep green-coloured ferns. She peered upwards at the azure sky and wondered if Knox had yet managed to trace their progress.

Were they being watched now via satellite?

She blinked the thought away, picking up her pace

to cross the clearing, and plunged into the thick wooded area on the other side.

An immediate coolness crossed her shoulders, thick pine trunks cluttering the path while her boots scuffed through needles and cones.

'Hang on. Piss break,' said Nathan, and wandered through the trees until he was out of sight.

Eva kicked at a stone, then peered along the path that lay before them, listening.

Apart from a pair of crows cawing from a branch farther back towards the clearing they'd just passed, the forest was silent.

'Can you trust this friend of yours?'

Eva stopped and turned to face Marie. 'With my life. What's with the questions?'

'Sorry – it's just that I've been chased by four men, and I've seen you kill them. I haven't seen my brother in years, I have no idea where we're going, who we're meeting, and one of my best friends is dead.' Marie took a deep breath, then uttered a bitter laugh. 'It's not like my training covered any of this.'

'It's a bit different when people die in front of you rather than from a few thousand metres up, is it?'

'That's not fair.'

'It never is.' Eva sighed. 'Look, there'll be time to grieve for Kelly when this is over. Right now, my job is to get us to this safe house of Decker's, find a way to get you to safety, and then find out what the bloody hell is going on.'

'Everything all right?' said Nathan, reappearing on the path.

'We're good.' She glanced at her wristwatch. 'We've got another four hours of daylight. I'd like to get to the outskirts of Deggendorf by then. I don't know about you two, but I don't fancy walking through here at night. Are you both going to be okay with that?'

Nathan nodded, and looked at his sister.

Marie shrugged. 'Lead the way.'

CHAPTER TWENTY-TWO

Five hours later, Eva crouched beside a high barbed wire fence surrounding an industrial estate on the fringes of the town.

The distant sound of evening traffic on the autobahn created a constant white noise, peppered with the occasional siren or blast from a truck horn. On the breeze, a chemical stench wafted across from one of the warehouses beyond the fence, the smells reminiscent of bleach and turpentine.

In the cool pale hues of the security lights dotted around the complex, tall thin chimneys poked up into the night sky belching steam and worse.

They had spent the past hour hovering at the fringes of the forest, now little more than thin woodland beside the industrial estate, waiting for the sun to disappear over the horizon before she decided it was safe to move.

A few cars were still parked within the complex, and she'd already spotted two armed security guards patrolling within. A single searchlight completed an anti-clockwise sweep of the perimeter fence every few minutes, and she ducked as it crossed their position.

After it passed, she could see movement at the back of one of the buildings. A wide aluminium door began to rise, and then she heard a truck engine start up from within. Moments later, the vehicle rolled out, its headlights illuminating a figure who waved it forward.

Cameras were positioned on top of one of the lighting gantries outside the loading bays, and she was sure there would be more fixed to the sides of the buildings to cover all angles.

The theft of chemicals was becoming a lucrative industry on the black market, and it was evident that the owners of this complex were taking no chances, especially when a vehicle was leaving with a full load on board.

Eva glanced over her shoulder to make sure Nathan and Marie stayed amongst the shadows in her wake, then pointed to the exit road snaking away from the complex when they caught up with her.

'We're going to head down there. See the landscaping that's been put in? Those shrubs and whatever? When I say run, you go – keep low, in a crouch – and head for those. On your hands and knees and keep going when you get there, understand?'

They mumbled their agreement, and she turned back to the industrial site.

The searchlight was approaching again.

Holding up her hand, she counted down the seconds, then hissed a command.

'Go!'

She didn't wait to see if they were following or whether they were keeping up. She kept her focus on the landscaped border of the exit road and forced another burst of energy from her tired legs, then launched herself into the shrubbery.

Eva rolled to break her fall and began crawling.

Behind her, she heard a soft crunch followed by another as Nathan and Marie joined her, and she shot them a grim smile over her shoulder.

Despite her misgivings about the intelligence officer, she was proving to be as good as her brother when it came to taking orders.

Thank Christ the woman hadn't been in a civilian role like Nathan had been when they first met.

Two non-combatants would have been one hell of a risk to escape with.

She swivelled on her toes as they caught up with her. 'Okay?'

'Yes,' said Nathan.

Marie nodded, then peered over her shoulder at the sound of the truck approaching from the direction of the industrial estate.

Eva peered over the low hedge in time to see it winding its way between the buildings, then turned back to the exit.

'Okay, pay attention,' she whispered. 'We've got a camera to our right up there on that lamp post at the end of the exit road. When that truck gets here, it's got to turn right at the junction – it's a one-way system here, look. As soon as I give the command, we're heading left as fast as we can, got it?'

She didn't wait for their response, but turned to face the street beyond their position.

She briefly wondered if they should wait another hour – maybe it would be safer, maybe there were other security patrols wandering the industrial estate, maybe—

The truck bore down on them, engine rumbling, and then she heard it slow as it approached the junction.

One last look each way.

No movement.

No-one waiting to pounce the moment they broke cover.

'Now!'

The truck was turning, executing a slow curve as the driver guided it to the right.

She hoped his attention was taken by steering the large load, and that he would be busy watching his mirrors rather than the three people who were now running away from the complex.

No alarms sounded in the distance, and she slowed to a fast walk, feeling the strain in her leg muscles now.

'How much farther?' said Nathan, catching up with her, panting from the exertion.

She winked, then pointed at a single redbrick building behind a crumbling wall.

'We're here.'

CHAPTER TWENTY-THREE

Miles rubbed at tired eyes, then reached out for the desk lamp and angled it onto the reports strewn across his desk.

The bright glow created a halo over his work and cast a sheen across the silver-framed photograph of him and his wife on their honeymoon.

The grim realisation that the lines on his face were deeper than back then and a reflection of the stress caused by his job rather than laughter wasn't wasted on him as he tried to concentrate on the myriad of information he held in his hands.

He turned the page of the latest report from Prague, and sighed.

Czech police were blaming the slaying of four unknown men on a drugs deal gone wrong, the suggestion fed to them by one of the Section's tactical disinformation groups currently based in Hungary.

Miles was wondering what had been used to grease the palms of who when he heard a noise out in the corridor.

He glanced up at a knock on the open door to see Greg hovering at the threshold.

The analyst held up a handful of stapled pages and a manila folder. 'I've got the information you were after about Marie Weston and the rest of our drone crew.'

'Come on in.' Miles waved him to one of the seats opposite his desk. 'That was quick.'

Greg grimaced. 'One of the few benefits of being a small agency, I guess. Besides, Knox was in his office and ran off the résumés for me. It saved me working through layers of security in the database instead.'

'Good thinking. How's it going out there with regard to finding out who the driver was who picked them up in Lincoln?'

'Nothing so far.' The analyst wrinkled his nose. 'Something – or someone – fucked up the CCTV coverage in the town centre where the restaurant is, so we've got no footage of the actual grab.'

'Shit.' Miles threw his pen on the desk. 'Any idea who?'

'Not yet. Jason's working through that at the moment to see if he can find a trace in the system to find out how it was hacked.'

'Keep me posted on that.'

'Will do. There is one thing, though – whoever tampered with the CCTV footage only removed the images from that night.' Greg tried, and failed to suppress a grin like the Cheshire cat. 'I think I might have something from the last time the crew went there, though.'

'What?'

'Yeah. I sent a message through to Nathan and asked him if his sister could confirm whether the restaurant was a favourite of theirs, and if so when they last went there.' He flipped open the folder in his lap and handed over a blown-up black and white photograph. 'I checked, and that car was parked outside six weeks ago, which correlates with the date Marie gave to Nathan.'

Miles sat forward and held the photograph closer under the lamp's beam. 'Registration number?'

'Stolen plates.'

'What about the driver? Any clearer shots than this?'

'None, but I'm not giving up yet. Now that we have a date, I've tasked Emily with running surveillance on all cameras in the area that night to see if we can spot the car and get a better image of the driver.' Greg took back the photograph Miles held out and tucked it into the file. 'Once we have that, we'll run him through the system.'

'That's great work, Greg.'

'We got lucky, that's all.'

Miles wasn't going to argue with the man. Anyone who could coerce three aircrew into a strange vehicle and then have them fly a stolen drone under the impression it was a sanctioned flight didn't plan for mistakes like that.

'What about Jeffrey Dukes? What've you managed to find out about him?'

Greg sighed and tossed the manila folder onto the desk between them. 'That's where things get weird.'

'How so?'

'Well, obviously there's everything you'd expect on the FCO system about him – role, who he reports to, achievements and all of that – but when I started to do some digging, it turns out no-one can remember what he was doing prior to joining the department. I can't even find out when he applied for the role.'

Miles frowned, pulled his keyboard across the desk towards him and typed in search string. He leaned back in his chair, his jaw set.

Greg was right.

No-one known as Jeffrey Dukes had applied for a role with the Foreign and Commonwealth Office.

Ever.

'Universities?' he suggested. 'Recruitment agency databases?'

'No, nothing there either.'

'What about a wider search?' Miles asked the analyst. 'National crime databases, MI6, GCHQ—'

'I already looked,' said Greg. 'Discreetly, of course. None of them will ever know I was there.'

'And?'

The analyst shrugged, his brow creased. 'That's what I'm trying to tell you. There was nothing in any of the systems about him. Nothing at all.'

'That's impossible.'

'That's what I said to Emily, but I've checked all the data. Outside of the Foreign and Commonwealth Office, Jeffrey Dukes never existed.'

CHAPTER TWENTY-FOUR

Eva leaned against the chipped plasterwork wall and released the magazine from her gun, running her thumb over the remaining bullets.

Shooting two of their pursuers in Prague had been a necessity, but she frowned at the memory.

She would much rather have killed them quietly, without raising the alarm or highlighting their position to their enemies.

At least the other two men were dispatched with little fuss.

Grabbing the knife from the kitchen drawer before leaving the flat had been a last-minute decision, a gut feeling, that was all – but it may have saved their lives.

Given that Miles and his team of analysts had managed to track them so easily through the city using

CCTV cameras, she had no doubt that others would have been watching as well.

But who did the four gunmen report to?

Who was controlling all of this?

And, why?

Sighing, she rested her head against the cool wall, closing her eyes for a moment.

Nathan and Marie had found four canvas cots at the back of the building in a store cupboard and now slept while she took the last watch for the night.

Both of them had been exhausted by the time they entered the disused telephone exchange, the security panel hidden on a metal post a few metres away yielding to the six digit code she'd entered on Decker's advice.

She didn't trust either of them to stay alert after the trek through the woods and so had remained on guard through to the early hours of the morning.

This was the dead time – the time when any attack on their position was most likely. The time when people naturally let down their defences and succumbed to REM sleep and deep dreams.

She opened her eyes as Nathan snuffled in his sleep and rolled over in the narrow cot, before she bit back a yawn and wandered across to a low desk set against one wall under a flight of concrete steps.

The basement wasn't ideal – there were damp patches up the walls and a distinct smell of mould from one of the vents in the corner – but it was out of sight and the upstairs level remained deserted, the original exchange equipment abandoned and dusty. The basement itself was only accessible through a heavy steel door, no doubt retrofitted by Decker at some point in recent years.

The older assassin had also installed a suite of powerful computer servers that hummed in the corner, providing a constant white noise to accompany Nathan's gentle snoring.

Four screens provided 24/7 coverage of the area around the telephone exchange, recording and storing the footage to an encrypted cloud-based drive for future reference.

Eva ran her gaze across the images, taking in the weed-covered and cracked concrete apron outside the building, and the road winding past on its way to the inner core of the industrial estate, then concentrated on the three buildings surrounding the old exchange in a C-shape.

Every now and again, an articulated truck would rumble past on its way to the chemical plant up the road but none of them had seen any other activity since their arrival.

She pulled out her encrypted mobile phone and peered at the screen, willing Decker to call.

She didn't want to do this on her own.

It was too much, with too many unknown factors.

Too risky.

She spun around and raised the gun at movement behind her, then swallowed as Nathan's eyes widened, his hands raised.

'It's only me.'

'Shit, sorry.' Eva lowered the gun. 'I thought you were asleep.'

'I was. I could hear you thinking, though.'

She gave him a gentle push and held her breath as the sound of another truck reached her ears.

Turning to the screens, she watched as the cab entered the screen first, then the long trailer it pulled, the headlights piercing a fine mist clinging to the road.

She choked out a gasp as something moved at the back of the truck – a fleeting silhouette that emerged from the rear and rolled to the floor before disappearing into the shadows.

Beside her, Nathan reached out for the keyboard and hit the pause button while the live recording continued on another screen. 'Did you see that?'

'Yeah. Someone was hitching a ride.' Eva was already heading towards the steps. 'Marie, rise and shine – we're about to have company, and it might not be friendly.'

The intelligence officer rolled over and rubbed at her eyes before sitting up and throwing back the covers, tugging her boots on as Eva's words sank in.

Eva flipped off the light switch at the bottom of the steps. 'Keep your voices down.'

'Is it Decker?' Nathan hissed.

Eva hugged the wall, keeping her gun lowered in a two-handed grip as she ascended. 'I bloody hope so. Otherwise, we're really in the shit.'

Reaching the top of the steps, she entered the security code and pressed her hand against the cold surface.

It swung open on well-oiled hinges and she blinked to counteract the final effects of the darkness enveloping her.

A tiny square window in the ceiling of the exchange provided some light, a pale early morning hue beginning to illuminate the old desks and electronics left behind by the telephone company – perhaps the CIA. Dust motes hung in the air as she gently pushed the door shut behind her and then dropped to a crouch.

Crawling over the concrete floor, using her elbows rather than her hands for fear of slicing them open on broken glass, she edged closer to the door.

There was only one way in, and one way out.

If someone had found their location, if someone was determined to silence Marie, then they were cornered.

Eva swallowed.

It was up to her to protect them.

She thumbed off the safety catch on the gun, and waited.

CHAPTER TWENTY-FIVE

Robert Nivens grimaced as he raised his chin and eyed the blue silk tie he knotted at the base of his neck.

'Darling? Your car will be here in twenty minutes.'

His wife's voice carried up the stairs over the dulcet tones of the Radio 4 morning broadcasters, prickling at his conscience.

'I know.' He peered at the pale reflection in the mirror and in that moment swore he would never agree to drinks with Marcus Trescothick again.

The Home Secretary had a reputation as a hard drinker and Robert's headache was bearing testimony to that, despite the two painkillers he had swallowed dry an hour ago upon waking.

Turning from the en suite sink, he padded into the bedroom and blinked in the cool sunlight beginning to stream through the floor-to-ceiling window at the far end.

Beyond the net curtain, a small balcony hung over secluded gardens surrounded by tall poplar trees. A squirrel bounded across the lawn, scampered past the children's croquet set and shot up a trellis beside a bird bath.

'Do you want another coffee?'

God, yes.

'Please, love.'

'Up there?'

'I'll be down in a second.'

Reaching down to loosen his belt buckle a notch, Robert crossed to the wardrobe and pulled a dark grey jacket from a hanger before lacing up his shoes and heading downstairs.

Deborah stood at the granite worktop next to the toaster, a glass of orange juice in her hand. She cocked an eyebrow when she saw him and turned down the volume on the digital radio.

'Best tell them you think you're coming down with a cold.'

'It could be.' He shot her a wan smile, placed the jacket on the back of one of the bar stools surrounding the central worktop and sank into one next to it.

'Plenty of water this morning – you'll feel fine by noon.' She pushed a steaming mug of coffee towards him, along with a plate on which two slices of marmalade-laden toast sat. 'What time's your meeting with the PM?'

'Ten.'

'Ah.'

'Indeed.' He took a sip of coffee, relishing the bitter taste that mingled with a satisfying sugar hit that smacked his back teeth. 'Remind me next time not to agree to drinks mid-week.'

'I did, after the last time. You never listen to me.'

'Pardon?'

She slapped his arm as she passed with the tea towel in her hand, and leaned against the kitchen doorframe. 'You two better be getting up,' she called. 'I'm leaving in half an hour.'

Robert raised his gaze to the ceiling as feet thumped on the floorboards above, and shook his head. 'One of these days, both of them will make it out of bed without being yelled at.'

'I wonder.' Deborah returned to the worktop and pulled out a chair beside him, reaching for his hand. 'Have you heard anything from Jeffrey yet?'

He shook his head. 'No. I'm beginning to worry, to be honest. The meetings he was scheduled to have were over and done with four days ago. He called the office and we spoke about the amended agenda for the talks next month, and he said he was getting a flight back two days ago.'

'And nothing since?'

'No.'

'What is the office doing about it?'

'As much as they can, in the circumstances.' He grimaced. 'The problem is of course, he's in the middle of bloody nowhere. Crap phone signal, little by way of internet connection…'

'Surely his driver would know where he is?'

'We can't get hold of him, either.'

'Oh.'

'I'll have Sally phone the local diplomatic missions again this morning – you know what she's like. She has contacts in most embassies outside of the usual suspects.' He forced a reassuring smile. His secretary had a formidable reputation, but he feared even this task would test her. 'And of course, the hospitals.'

Deborah wrinkled her nose. 'God, I hope he's okay. He seemed such a lovely man when he was here for the party last month.'

'Very dependable.' Robert drained his coffee and picked up his jacket and briefcase at the sound of a car pulling up outside. 'Which is why this is such unusual behaviour for him.'

'You haven't eaten your toast, darling.'

'Give it to Joshua,' he said, and kissed her cheek as their eldest son appeared.

'Ugh, gross,' said the teenager, collecting his father's plate and wandering off in the direction of the living room.

'Sit down while you're eating,' Debbie called after him. She turned to Robert, reached out and straightened his tie while he shrugged on his jacket. 'And you – take some more painkillers in a couple of hours. I'm sure you'll be fine.'

'Right.'

A cold morning chill nipped at his ears when he opened the front door and hurried down the steps to the waiting car.

His driver opened the back door and nodded. 'Morning, Foreign Secretary.'

'Morning, Stephen.'

'Heating's on, sir, and the traffic report isn't too bad.'

'Good to hear, thank you.'

Robert settled onto the back seat as the door swung shut, then opened the briefcase and extracted a sheaf of paperwork.

It was twenty minutes before he blinked and looked up from the draft report, and noticed the familiar black wrought-iron railings and Georgian frontage of Downing Street properties. He pressed the intercom button.

'What's going on, Stephen? Why aren't we at Portcullis House per my schedule?'

'Sorry, Foreign Secretary,' came the reply. 'Urgent meeting convened by the Prime Minister for eight o'clock sharp. The call just came through.'

Robert frowned. 'Did they say what it was about?'

The driver's eyes met his in the rear-view mirror, and he shook his head. 'Above my pay grade, sir.'

The Foreign Secretary shoved the paperwork back in his briefcase, his heart rate missing a beat.

What was going on?

CHAPTER TWENTY-SIX

Eva bit back a curse as a shard of metal tore into her elbow, picked out the remnants of a broken transistor with her fingernails, then shuffled closer to the door.

Her breathing was shallow now, controlled, with any fear battened down and shoved away.

She had a job to do.

Reaching the wall beside the entrance, she paused to listen.

There was movement from outside – whoever was approaching the building was well-trained, and patient.

She stared at the floor, her mind recalling the layout beyond the door.

Tall weeds, abandoned rusting equipment, rotting plywood cable reels – plenty of places to hide.

Her head jerked up as the lock mechanism released,

and the barrel of a gun appeared through a gap in the door.

'If you're pointing a weapon at me, Delacourt, now would be a good time to lower it,' came a laconic voice.

'Decker?'

She exhaled as a tall figure slipped into the room and shut the door, then checked her gun was safe before walking over to him and slapping his arm. 'You scared the shit out of me.'

He shifted a canvas sports bag onto his shoulder, then tucked his own gun under his leather jacket. 'Think of it as free training.'

Despite the gloom, she could hear the smile in his voice. 'I could do without it at the moment.'

'Sounds like you've been busy, Delacourt.'

'Prague?'

'Prague. It's all over the wires. Do you know who they were?'

She shook her head. 'Not yet. We're hoping Miles and Knox might be able to tell us more when we call them.'

Leading the way over to the basement door, she paused with her hand hovering above the security panel and turned. 'I'm glad you're here.'

He said nothing, and gestured to the concrete steps.

The lights flashed to life as she began to descend, and Nathan peered up at them from his position next to the computer screens, his arms crossed over his chest.

'Found him, then?'

'Good to see you too, nerd.' Decker thrust out his hand and shook Nathan's before turning to Marie. 'I presume you're the one who started all this.'

'I—'

'This is my sister, Marie,' said Nathan.

'Figures.' Decker sank into one of the chairs beside the screens and dropped the bag onto the floor.

It landed with a soft clang of metal and something else.

Eva raised an eyebrow. 'Supplies?'

'Supplies.' He leaned over and unzipped the bag, rummaged inside, then thrust an M4 carbine at her. 'Figured these would be better. Good at close quarters, as well as a reasonable distance.'

She took the weapon from him, sighted it at the far wall and then handed it to Nathan. 'How many did you bring?'

'Two of these, plus four pistols and plenty of ammunition. That okay?'

'Perfect.' Eva leaned over, picked up one of the smaller guns and a box of ammunition, and then crossed over to where Marie hovered beside her brother. 'Here. I presume you can use it?'

'Yes.' Marie held out her hand for the rounds, then thumbed them into the empty magazine. 'Hopefully I won't have to, right?'

'That's right,' said Decker, then turned to the others.

'You said you were waiting to hear from Miles and Knox?'

'We thought it better to wait until you got here,' said Nathan. 'In case you think of anything we should ask – at the moment, you know as much as we do.'

'Don't hang about then. Get them on the line.'

CHAPTER TWENTY-SEVEN

'We've found the driver who kidnapped Marie and her crew.'

Miles's voice echoed off the walls of the basement, and Eva's breath caught in her throat.

'Who is he?' she said, leaning forward on one of the chairs they had pulled into a semi-circle around the computer screens. 'What has he told you?'

'Nothing,' said Knox, his mouth twisting. 'He's dead.'

'Fuck.' Decker crossed his arms over his chest and leaned against the wall, away from the camera's lens.

Unlike Eva and Nathan, he had no agreement with the Section regarding amnesty arrangements, and wasn't prepared to risk them seeing what he looked like these days. He ran a hand over his lantern jaw and sighed. 'Did you kill him?'

'Don't be ridiculous,' Knox snapped. 'Our team of analysts traced the car through the Automatic Number Plate Recognition system to a car park above a beach in Sussex. His body was at the bottom of a cliff.'

'Pushed?' said Marie. 'Or did he jump?'

'Throat slit, fingers missing, then pushed,' said Miles. 'Somebody decided he wasn't useful anymore.'

'Or figured out that he'd screwed up getting caught on CCTV a week before the crew were picked up,' said Knox. 'Either way, we have no other leads on him or his acquaintances.'

'Did the car appear on any other CCTV or ANPR cameras after he picked us up from the restaurant?' said Marie. 'I mean, we went from there straight to the airfield.'

'In which direction?' said Knox.

'East.' Marie frowned. 'He used side streets to get out of the city. We went through Wragby before he turned north – it was just country lanes after that. No villages or anything. The airfield we were flown out of was in the middle of nowhere, but I mean that's not unusual is it? You've done the same when we've flown—'

Knox held up his hand to silence her. 'There's no requirement to mention other missions here. I take your point, though – we're looking for somewhere that a private plane can enter and leave the country without having to file a flight plan but so far, we've got nothing.'

'And the driver managed to avoid the CCTV and ANPR cameras on the night he collected you,' added Miles. 'The ones near the restaurant were vandalised, and he knew where the others were by then. We haven't spotted the car anywhere else.'

'What about this Jeffrey Dukes?' said Eva. 'What can you tell us about him?'

'Outside of his Foreign Office career, there's nothing,' he said, a note of defeat in his voice. 'Again, we've discreetly gone through all other intelligence agencies' records but the man's—'

'A spook,' said Decker, then shrugged as Eva twisted around to look at him. 'Has to be, right?'

'That's what we beginning to suspect,' said Knox. 'Zero past prior to working for Robert Nivens.'

'What about present history?' Nathan said. 'What *do* you know about him?'

'We sent someone over to the FCO on the pretence of wanting to speak to him – they said Dukes was due to arrive on a flight from Ankara yesterday morning according to one of the administrative team. And,' said Miles, flicking open a file on the desk beside him, 'he's rumoured to be in a relationship with one of the other admin team members – a woman by the name of Charlotte Hughes.'

'What information do you have on her?' said Eva.

'Career civil servant, divorced, keeps to herself – nothing on social media.' Miles slapped the folder shut. 'We'll keep a watching brief in case anyone tries to contact her.'

'If Jeffrey Dukes is a spook, who's he working for?' said Decker.

'We don't know that he is yet.'

'Hurry, then. We need to find out what – who – we're up against,' said the older assassin. 'And what the threats are.'

'What are our next steps?' said Eva. 'We can't stay where we are forever. We need to do something.'

'Decker – can you get Marie to the airfield at Rosenheim by six o'clock tonight?' said Miles.

'You try anything, Newcombe, I'll—'

'We're not interested in bringing you back here,' said Knox, his tone impatient. 'Think of this as a temporary reprieve – we can have that conversation at a later date.'

'This is about getting Marie to safety,' said Miles, then turned his attention to the intelligence officer. 'We're sending over a private charter to bring you back here – that way, you can give us an in-depth account of what happened in case we've missed anything, and work with the team here. Between now and your extraction time, you need to help Nathan try to identify the other personnel you saw at the airfield in Belarus.'

'Okay,' said Marie. She shoved her hands in the

pockets of her sweatshirt. 'I've been making some notes here, too – a map of the layout of the airfield so we can try to source that through satellite imagery.'

'Good work. Our primary goal is to identify and trace the man posing as your commanding officer through other people he's been associating with.'

'Whoever this man is, he's managed to keep his identity hidden from every single UK intelligence agency I've spoken to,' said Knox. 'Unless we can identify him and get a clear image, we can't use facial recognition software to run a check on passengers through worldwide airports, either. I've spoken with my contacts at the NSA and CIA, and he's a complete unknown to them as well – they're not aware of any operations running out of Belarus.'

'Are you sure he's not one of them?' said Decker. 'He's sounds like an evil son of a bitch – just the sort of person they like.'

'I've only got their word for it,' said Knox.

Decker snorted.

'Which still doesn't address the question – why use the drone to kill Dukes?' said Miles.

'You're right.' Eva leaned back in her chair. 'It seems extreme – not to mention risky, doesn't it? I mean why not simply pay one of the local militia to use a rocket launcher? Or someone like me to poison him?'

She heard Nathan swallow before he shook his head and shrugged.

'What?' she said. 'It would've been easier to arrange, and less likely to cause attention if he used an assassin, wouldn't it?

Marie paced the floor, her arms wrapped around her middle. 'What if…?'

She shook her head.

'Spit it out,' Decker growled.

'What if the man posing as Colonel Richards killed him that way to make a point? What if Dukes found out that Richards was up to something?' The intelligence officer paused and faced the small group. 'It's just that, if the drone we were using *was* stolen, or decommissioned before being stolen en route to being scrapped, and Richards needed to show someone that it was in working order, then perhaps he saw a way to do so—'

'—by demonstrating its capabilities and killing the one man who might have been threatening his whole organisation if he'd stumbled across it,' Eva finished. 'Jeffrey Dukes.'

A shocked silence filled the basement before Nathan cleared his throat.

'Whoever Colonel Paul Richards is, then like Decker says he's one seriously evil screwed-up son of a bitch.'

CHAPTER TWENTY-EIGHT

Eva bit back a yawn and peered at the screen in front of her through blurred vision before rubbing her eyes.

An aroma of olive oil filled the basement as Decker broke apart each of the weapons he had arrived with and gave each a thorough clean, his movements methodical and unhurried.

'I thought you said you grew grapes,' said Nathan, tearing his attention away from the second screen that he and Marie were working on.

'I sell the grapes. I keep the olives.' Decker shrugged. 'It's not as good as the proper stuff for cleaning these, but less likely to draw attention.'

Marie stifled a laugh.

'What?'

'You've arrived with a sack full of handguns and

assault rifles. I don't think anyone would be worrying about gun oil if you'd been caught.'

The corner of Decker's mouth twitched, but then he frowned and turned his attention to Eva.

'When did you last sleep?'

She blinked. 'I don't know – two days ago, perhaps?'

'Get your head down. You're no use to them tired.'

'He's right,' said Nathan. 'We can carry on with this.'

'I'm fine.' Eva held up her hand to ward off the next retort as he opened his mouth. 'Don't worry – I'll sleep when Decker takes Marie to the airfield. You can keep watch and wake me if anyone shows up. How're you doing with the satellite images?'

Nathan sighed. 'I've managed to download some standard imagery off the internet, but it's not brilliant. I'd be happier if we had some up-to-date ones to work from but I can't find anyone with a spare satellite to pass over that area. They're too busy watching the South China Sea and North Africa for the next two days. It'll take half that time just to request the necessary clearances.'

'Okay, well it's quiet outside at the moment and there's nothing on our security cameras here, so send the files over to me. Marie, give me that map of yours. You two keep going with the photofits. We're in danger of running out of time before you have to leave otherwise, and I want to make a move first thing in the morning.'

Eva turned back to her screen, spread out Marie's map on the desk next to her and opened up the image files sent over from London.

After taking a swig from a bottle of water, she pulled her chair closer to the screen and peered at each of the images in turn. Despite Nathan's best efforts to clean them up, the contours and features were pixelated and distorted beyond recognition in some places until she found a setting that enabled her to easily scan the pastures and woodland peppering the landscape.

With Marie's careful notations of the places she had passed on her way out of the country, Eva could narrow down the area to a set of grid references to the south of the country and work her way west.

It didn't take long to find a potential candidate.

Her knowledge of Belarusian history was scant but she recalled the way the country had been used as a strategic frontline operation throughout the Cold War, so when she opened the fourth satellite image and noticed a deep scar through a forest just north of the Ukrainian border, her gut twisted.

'Marie? How long does the runway need to be for a Reaper to take off safely?'

The intelligence officer wrinkled her nose. 'About 5,000 feet but that's when it's fully loaded. I reckon the one we used was much shorter than that – maybe 3,000 feet, perhaps less. Why?'

She wandered across to where Eva was working, and leaned over to look at the screen.

Eva grinned. 'I think I've found it. Does any of this look familiar to you?'

Marie dragged her chair over, Decker joining them as Eva enlarged the area and tried to adjust the settings.

'That's as close as I can get,' she said, pushing the mouse away. 'Well?'

'These are the two hangars I remember,' said Marie, and tapped the screen, unable to keep the excitement from her voice. 'The runway is about the right length, and – look – this boundary here is where the command centre was set up. This must be the way Kelly and I ran after Josh…'

She broke off, and Decker put his hand on her shoulder.

'We'll pay them back for what they did to all of you, I promise. But right now, you need to tell us as much as possible about this place. Where's the command centre? I can't see it in this photo.'

'This image is over a year old,' said Eva, peering at the screen.

Marie sniffed. 'The command centre is … it's like a shipping container. That's the best way I can describe it. About the same size too. I didn't get the impression it had been there long either because it was still on a trailer.'

'Did you get the licence plate on the trailer?' said Decker.

'I didn't see one on it, and there were no logos or names of haulage companies along the sides,' said Marie, frowning. 'They'd put up some temporary metal steps for us to get in and out of the command centre. I can't remember seeing a truck or a crane anywhere on the airfield so I think they were just leaving it set up like that.'

Decker turned to Eva. 'We need to go there. For a start, we need to destroy that Reaper – and if we can't find it, then destroying the command centre is our next best option.'

'We'll make a start tomorrow after Marie's out of the country safely,' she said.

Nathan glanced at his sister as he began scrolling through photographs again. 'We'll probably be done with this in another hour. There aren't many—'

'Wait.' Marie moved her chair across and stabbed her finger at his screen. 'Him. That's the Colonel. I recognise him. He was talking to another man when we were driven across the airfield from the plane after we landed. They were standing outside the door to the command centre when the car stopped.'

'Did you get a name?' said Eva.

The intelligence officer shook her head. 'I didn't, but as we got out of the car he smiled at the Colonel, then got a lift back towards the hangars at the far end of the airfield before we went inside the command centre to start our mission.'

'Okay, good – that's something,' said Nathan. 'We'll flag him and pass that image on to Miles and his team. Let's keep going and see if you recognise anyone else.'

'Stop.'

Eva looked up from her screen as Decker's voice echoed off the walls.

Nathan's hand froze above the mouse before he recovered. 'What?'

'Go back.' Decker pointed at the screen, his tone impatient. 'Scroll back to that last image.'

He stood with his arms across his chest as a face reappeared, and let out a satisfied grunt. 'I know him. The Colonel.'

Nathan's eyes narrowed. 'In what capacity?'

'Professional, of course.'

'From where?' said Eva. 'Or, should I say – when?'

'About eight years back, in the Philippines. I did some freelance work outside of the Section for the FBI. Or someone associated with them.' Decker's jaw tightened. 'They took over six months to pay up.'

'Never mind that,' said Nathan, his tone urgent. 'Who the hell is he?'

'Sean Tozer. Another freelancer. Nasty piece of shit, too. I was glad to see the back of him.'

Marie looked from him to Eva. 'Do assassins have an ethics code?'

'Of sorts.' Eva frowned. 'Have you heard from him or seen him since, Decker?'

'No – you know what it's like.'

'True.' She peered back at the screen as Nathan continued to scroll through image after image, the database now displaying a shortened search string. 'What about ground crew, Marie? Recognise anyone else?'

'Not yet,' Marie murmured, nibbling at a thumbnail. 'Keep going.'

Eva held her breath.

'There!'

Nathan froze as Marie leaned forward, her eyes blazing.

On the screen, a swarthy-looking man was shaking hands with an unidentified woman, her back to the camera. The man wore a smart suit, his jawline sculpted with a closely-cropped beard. He wore a smile, but it didn't reach his eyes.

'Says here he goes by the name of Aaron Sykes,' said Eva, running her gaze down the scant information the Section's database had gathered. 'No known connections to terrorist organisations though.'

'I saw him there,' said Marie. 'That's the man I said was talking to the Colonel when we got to the airfield.'

'Perfect.' Eva patted Nathan's shoulder. 'Now we have a location, and two names.'

'And, if we have names, we have targets,' added Decker, then grinned. 'That's an improvement.'

CHAPTER TWENTY-NINE

Charlotte clipped back her long fringe, shrugged a sweatshirt over her shoulders and walked through the flat to the compact open-plan kitchen and living area.

She eyed the post that had been waiting for her in the mailbox downstairs when she arrived home, then reached out and discarded the pamphlets and brochures from food delivery services and the local pizza place in a small recycling box near the front door. She pushed the remainder to one side before tugging the padded envelope from her bag instead.

Pouring a generous measure of Pinot Noir into a glass, she wandered over to the sofa and placed the envelope on a low table in front of her.

She hadn't had a chance to go through what Jeffrey had sent to her yet.

One look at his note at the office and she had scurried back to her desk while Hodges was ending his call, and shoved the envelope and its contents into her bag before kicking it under her desk out of sight.

She couldn't get home fast enough.

The tube journey back to Finsbury Park had passed by in a blur, her movements automatic, and then as she'd twisted the key in the lock to her front door, the excitement had swelled.

She took a sip of the wine, then put down the glass and pulled the contents from the envelope.

A folded map fell out between the loose pages and slid to the floor between her feet. Scrambling for it with her left hand, she flipped it over and emitted a surprised snort.

'What were you doing in Syria? You were supposed to be in Turkey…'

She tried to recall what she knew about the place – war-torn, rampant starvation and a refugee crisis that no longer reached the headlines in England.

A forgotten country.

Running her thumb over the map, she blinked at the red biro Xs next to two locations and held it closer.

There were no town names beside the markings, no roads twisting over the contours.

Nothing.

She shook her head and dropped the map on top of

the envelope and turned her attention to the papers in her right hand.

The pages looked as if they had been ripped out of an A5-sized notebook, Jeffrey's scrawl just about legible across the fine lines. Page numbers had been pre-printed in the bottom right-hand corner, and Charlotte realised that he had torn them from the middle of the notebook – pages one through thirty and then fifty-three and beyond were missing.

Frowning as she flicked through them, she concluded that the numbers he'd written down resembled global positioning system coordinates and the accompanying text – some of the ink blurred with sweat from Jeffrey's fingers by the look of it – included descriptions of people, men he had seen at those locations.

Two men, but no names.

Charlotte flipped over the final pages clipped together – A4 sheets this time, with a hotel logo on the top – and frowned as she read the text beneath.

Jeffrey's handwriting looped across the pages, as if he had been taking hurried notes while on the phone to someone – there were bullet points running haphazardly down the left hand side, and then scribbled questions on the right, with arrows to other thoughts he had jotted down. A date and time appeared at the top of the second page she turned to, and she frowned as she realised it was dated three days ago, when she had expected him back in Ankara and a phone call to say he would be back in London soon.

Instead, the word "İzmir" had been written in capital letters, and underlined twice.

Charlotte lowered the pages and reached out for the wineglass, taking a sip while she mulled over the details.

Jeffrey's hurried scrawl spoke of a compromised arms shipment. Somehow, he had identified that four missiles had been stolen in Malta before the ship continued its journey to İzmir, and a corresponding rogue drone that he was now chasing.

The emergency meeting convened with the heads of the intelligence services had taken place two days ago, and a flurry of activity followed while Edward Toskins' staff tried to throw together a report that would mitigate any blame for the missing weapons from the original shipment that left the USA.

For the shipment contained a sale agreed by the Department for International Trade.

Except from the reports Charlotte had seen in the past twenty-four hours, and the conversations she'd overheard between Hodges and Toskins, there had been no mention of the missing Hellfire missiles, or whether the theft was a one-off occurrence.

Everyone in the department was at a loss as to how the weapons had been stolen, especially as the container had been sealed prior to its original departure.

How did someone break into the container, steal the missiles and then re-seal it without being seen?

And what of the two men described in the torn pages from Jeffrey's notebook?

Why didn't he have their names?

Hadn't he been introduced to them?

If not, why not?

His position as special adviser to the Foreign Secretary had led to the hastily arranged assignment. Some sort of panic that had Jeffrey rolling his eyes as he'd told her over a late dinner and explained that he would be leaving for Ankara.

That had been over a week ago, and she hadn't heard from him since.

She even tried phoning the woman who made all the department's travel arrangements, only to be told that Jeffrey had insisted on making his own arrangements. Unusual, but as he was an advisor rather than a minister of Her Majesty's Government and not regarded as a security risk, she had acquiesced.

Afterwards, she tried to find a copy of his itinerary beyond the busy international airport, but there was nothing, not even a hotel name or car rental company.

Once he had arrived in Turkey, there was a void.

Dukes had disappeared without a trace.

Now, this.

Her heart leapt as her mobile vibrated on the coffee

table a split second before a Rolling Stones track blasted out.

'What do you want?'

'Ouch. How are you?'

Charlotte's gaze ran over the paperwork strewn across the table and she sighed. 'Confused. Sorry. What about you?'

'Turn on the TV.'

Her brother's urgent tone had her reaching for the remote control on the arm of the sofa before she thought to ask why.

'Where are you?' she said as she aimed the remote at the TV in the corner and waited for the menu to display.

'The airport. Put it on the BBC. You need to see this.'

There was noise in the background – people shouting to each other, loud music, laughter.

'Are you in the bar?' she said, selecting the 24-hour news channel.

'Have you got it on yet?'

Charlotte didn't answer.

Instead, she dropped the remote, then clutched the phone in shaking hands as her brother's voice carried through the speaker.

On the television, the image changed from a news studio to a dusty landscape and a world-worn male reporter faced the camera. His voice echoed the words flashing past on a red-coloured ticker tape along the bottom of the screen, the text screaming out at her.

Foreign Secretary's representative Jeffrey Dukes suffers heart attack while in Turkey for Syrian peace talks.

CHAPTER THIRTY

Ankara

Adrian Ogilvy lowered his sunglasses onto his nose and rolled up his cotton shirt sleeves as he left the hotel, unaware that he was being watched.

In his mid-sixties, he walked at the pace of a man with purpose, and of one for whom exercise was a regular occurrence.

He checked his watch, the timepiece gleaming in the bright light already causing sweat to prickle at his hairline. He had an hour until the pre-arranged meeting but wanted to arrive early in order to assess the location.

His contact – Mahdi – had suggested a remote location for their meeting, and Adrian had readily agreed. It was far away from the diplomatic quarter, away from prying ears and eyes, and the drive would serve to give him time to batten down his increasing panic.

Adrian's gaze shot to his left as double glass doors parted and a waft of air-conditioned coolness swept over him.

Most people – particularly the tourists – were sensible enough to spend the daylight hours by the hotel pool or visiting one of the malls to stay out of the heat.

He did not have the luxury of choice.

Not now.

His attention snapped to the right as a convoy of black limousines passed, the licence plates revealing the passengers to be diplomats behind the smoked-out windows before the cars swept by and turned through the gates to one of the many embassies lining the streets in the city.

A cursory glance over his shoulder gave him no cause for concern.

Families congregated in small groups outside the shops – parents bickered in the midday heat, sulking children with bored expressions at their heels while women in niqabs hurried past clutching laden bags from the market and department stores. A long line of traffic curled along the road in both directions, the movement of the vehicles swift, busy while a siren wailed in the distance.

Adrian picked up his pace, wishing he'd

remembered to wear the straw fedora that was currently sitting on the middle of the hotel room's king-sized bed where he'd left it in his rush to leave.

Jaw set, he pulled a cotton handkerchief from his trouser pocket and wiped his forehead, then swallowed.

His heart rate was elevated, not from the exercise – he played tennis three times a week back home in England, and was used to working in the refugee camps based closer to the Equator – but from a nagging worry that had grown since a phone call last night.

He slowed as he approached a grey four-by-four parked at the kerb, aimed his key fob at it and threw himself behind the wheel, grateful for the tinted windows keeping out some of the heat. Starting the engine, he opened the windows until the air conditioning started to pump out a cool breeze, then swiped the parking permit off the dashboard and pulled into a gap in the traffic.

He thumbed down the volume on the steering wheel controls, the muted voices of the BBC World Service fading to the background, then shuffled in his seat as the vehicle in front ground to a halt at a set of lights and pulled his phone from his pocket. Once it was in its cradle beside the air vents, he checked the screen.

Still no new messages.

Fears confirmed, he exhaled and tried to order his jumbled thoughts.

His role as director for a non-government

organisation was one he had coveted since his late thirties, so when the opportunity presented itself fifteen years ago he had jumped at the chance. As with many charity workers, he remained of the optimistic belief that what he was doing made a difference, however small, to groups of people with no remaining hope.

He had spent his life since in the Middle East, not in places like Saudi Arabia or the United Arab Emirates but in the poorer countries – the ones that didn't have the immense oil and gas reserves of the neighbouring kingdoms and fiefdoms.

Adrian had been threatened, beaten up and shot at during his time with the NGO.

But this?

This was different.

He could anticipate the threats back then and chose to ignore them, risking his life to save others.

This time, he didn't know who he could trust.

Mahdi had been the first person he had contacted after the phone call in a desperate attempt to counter the claims made, his words carefully chosen and choked out staccato-like for fear of giving away too much in his state of panic.

Mahdi had a way of knowing things, finding out who knew what, and how to obtain information.

Adrian could only hope that the man had some answers for him now.

Taking a deep breath, he tore his attention away from the screen when the car in front surged forward.

It was only five minutes from here to the British Embassy if he turned back.

He had hoped the drive would serve to calm his nerves – except it hadn't, and now he didn't know what to do next or whether he would make the right decision.

Meet with Mahdi and report back, or take what he knew to the consulate and hope for the best?

His gaze moved to his phone again and he squinted at the last text message he had received.

I know it's been through here. Heading out to get us some evidence. See you in a couple of days.

He grimaced.

It had sounded so simple in hindsight, except now Jeffrey Dukes had disappeared off the face of the planet as far as his contact in Europe could deduce and no-one else could shed light on what had happened to him either.

Meanwhile, the UK government were pushing a bullshit story about Dukes suffering a heart attack while on FCO duties in Syria.

Adrian feared the worst.

They had known there would be risk. They had known it might come to this, but there had been hope for a fleeting moment.

Now with Jeffrey missing, feared dead, it was up to Adrian to take the next steps.

'Fuck it.' He slapped the wheel, indicated right, and took the exit.

As the city faded behind him, the desert reclaimed the highway. Sand shifted across the hot asphalt, whipped up by a wind that he knew could dehydrate a man in minutes.

After half an hour, he eased off the accelerator and braked when a worn sign riddled with bullet holes appeared on the left. He steered the four-by-four up a rough stony track that soon gave way to the fine grit of the desert, the suspension rocking the vehicle left and right as Adrian kept a firm grip on the steering wheel and negotiated the undulating landscape.

Rounding the curve of the next dune, he let out a breath he hadn't been aware he was holding when he saw the parked battered white car a little over half a mile away, its windscreen glinting in the midday sun.

A squat man wearing a long pale blue cotton shirt over black trousers raised his hand in greeting, and Adrian honked the horn in recognition, a sigh of relief passing his lips.

'Thank God,' he muttered.

The explosion obliterated the horizon.

One moment Mahdi was there beside his car, the next a burning wreckage lifted into the air before plummeting into a crater of sand that sent a plume of dust in all directions.

Adrian stomped on the brake pedal, the four-by-four

sliding to a standstill on the uneven surface while sand and stones peppered the windscreen, splintering the glass.

A wave of heat tore across the upholstery, Adrian's eyes wide as air was forced from his lungs by the shockwave.

Ears ringing from a piercing white noise tearing into his brain, he loosened his seat belt with shaking hands and stumbled from behind the wheel, dropping to the sand.

He cried out as his ankle twisted – then he was up, limping away from the four-by-four.

The crackle and pop of the fire tearing through what was left of Mahdi's car seemed distant, vague, and as he glanced over his shoulder, he whimpered.

They hadn't just killed Mahdi.

He had been annihilated.

Adrian tripped, then raised his gaze to the sky.

His hopes were fading, only to be replaced by a menacing terror growing closer every second.

'Please, God – no.'

He began to run, ignoring the searing pain shooting up his leg.

The second explosion threw him forward, his body limp as it slammed into the desert earth.

All the air was sucked from his lungs as the four-by-four disintegrated, a subsonic roar piercing his eardrums before his skin began to burn from the shrapnel tearing into his flesh.

He raised his head to scream, but no sound came.

As he tumbled to the ground, blood oozing from his nose and mouth, Adrian realised that his greatest fear was not of dying, but of what would happen next.

Because with both him and Jeffrey dead, it could only mean one thing.

His contact in Europe was the only one of them left, and what they were trying to stop was inevitable if he failed.

War.

CHAPTER THIRTY-ONE

Belarus

Eva hunkered beside Nathan and Decker and peered through a gap in a natural boundary of tangled brambles towards the clearing beyond the trees.

She grimaced as cramp threatened her calf muscles, her legs tired from the circuitous walk they had undertaken after ditching the car Decker had stolen on the outskirts of Deggendorf to get Marie to safety the night before.

They had set out as soon as he had returned from the airfield Knox had indicated, travelling along side streets and country lanes to pass through Germany into Poland and now, here.

A low sun warmed her neck, the horizon streaked

with indigo and orange as it set behind her, blinding anyone who might be facing towards them.

Decker dropped to his knees and motioned to her to do the same, Nathan at her heels.

'We'll get closer, take a look and then come up with a plan,' he murmured.

She nodded in response, then crawled through the undergrowth in his wake, their movements slow and meticulous.

Above her head, the tree canopy remained silent and a shiver crept over her shoulders at the peace enveloping them.

It made for slow progress, and she fought down the paranoia that they would be heard by whoever was patrolling the airfield.

Nathan had been quiet since they set out overnight, and she knew he was worried about his sister.

Marie would be safe in London all the time she was under the protection of the Section, but what would happen to her if they didn't stop whoever was responsible for ordering the murder of Jeffrey Dukes and stealing the Hellfire missiles?

Eva had tried her best to reassure him, telling him that Miles and Knox hadn't let him down before but she knew her words had fallen on deaf ears.

Nathan wouldn't rest until they had stopped the rogue Reaper and its new owner for good, and she wasn't going to let him down – or let him get hurt.

She owed him too much.

Ahead, Decker raised his hand and she stopped, listening.

Still that deathly silence.

Eva kept her eyes tracking the undergrowth as they passed, her keen senses alert to any hidden cameras or tripwires.

But there was nothing.

'This doesn't look good,' Decker murmured.

To her surprise, he rose to his feet and brushed off his jeans before holding out his hand to help her to her feet. Once Nathan had caught up, Decker reached forward and pushed back the final branches in their way.

'We're too late,' he said, and stepped into the clearing. 'Whoever they were, they've gone.'

Eva swore under her breath as they followed him, her gaze taking in the flat landscape stretching out from their position towards the tree line over a mile away.

To her right, half a mile from their position, two hulking metal skeletons reached up to the darkening sky, twisted and scorched.

'Those were the hangars Marie told us about, right?' said Nathan.

'I reckon so,' said Decker. He sniffed the air. 'That was recent, too. Can you smell it? Petrol.'

'It must've taken a hell of a lot of it to do that to two

hangars,' said Eva. 'I can't see anyone around – let's take a closer look.'

Despite the place looking abandoned, they circled the airfield rather than enter the clearing, approaching the still-smouldering remnants as the sun's rays dipped below the line of trees they had emerged from.

Small bats fluttered in the air, swooping on moths in the twilight by the time Eva reached the first hangar but she left the flashlight in her backpack alone.

Until they were sure no-one else was around, she didn't want to flag their position.

'What do you think?' she said as the others joined her.

'Whoever we're dealing with, he's thorough.'

'No shit.' She peered into the distance. 'No sign of a Reaper or the command centre, either. Do you think they broke camp right after killing Jeffrey?'

'If they did, how did they move the Reaper?' said Nathan. 'This landing strip isn't long enough for a transport plane.'

'They must've flown it out under cover of darkness,' said Decker. 'No need to worry about being seen on radar, either – they could fly at a low altitude for most of the time if they needed to.'

Eva reached out her hand and patted one of the corrugated iron panels that had crumpled from the heat. 'This is cold – I think they left days ago, rather than hours.'

'So we need to get onto London and have them track any trucks hauling shipping containers out of this area,' he said. 'At least they might be able to give us a direction, if not a final destination.'

'Not to mention finding out how the hell these people got their hands on the command centre in the first place,' said Nathan. 'I mean, it's one thing getting your hands on a drone if it crashed somewhere remote and was considered a write-off, but a whole command centre as well?'

'You'd be amazed how much kit goes missing after a retreat,' said Decker, his eyes glinting. 'How do you think I got my hands on half the stuff I store at home? All they'd have to do is break it up into smaller pieces of equipment and scatter it to the wind. Wouldn't take much.'

'How much would a Reaper be worth?' said Eva.

'I think the flyaway cost is a shade under sixteen million dollars,' said Nathan. 'I'm not aware of a resale cost but given that the RAF is phasing them out and replacing with the Protector generation of autonomous drones, I'll bet a few countries will be eyeing up the UK's existing stock of Reapers rather than having nothing at all.'

'How accurate are the records regarding Reapers that have been shot down in action or crashed?' said Decker.

'It's never been questioned before,' said Nathan,

rubbing his chin. 'That said, US and UK forces lose somewhere around twenty every year – that's more a reflection of how many missions are being flown these days rather than specific mechanical issues.'

'Still, if there's been a miscount at some point along the command chain or a Reaper went missing and was presumed destroyed…'

'Then that would explain how this rogue one ended up in the hands of a terrorist,' said Eva.

Nathan visibly shuddered. 'In which case, we have to keep a tight control on who knows about this until such time as we have those answers.'

'This is no time to play politics,' Decker growled. 'If someone's got hold of a drone and is using it to target and kill British citizens then a full audit of the write-offs needs to be done now. Not to mention who's got access to ordering missiles – or a way to steal them.'

Eva turned away from the airfield and eyed them both, her hands on her hips. 'There's a bigger problem we need to consider at the moment.'

'What's that?' said Nathan.

'Who's flying the drone now?'

CHAPTER THIRTY-TWO

Monaco

Elliott Wilder stood at the threshold to his office and squinted against the bright sunlight streaming into the room.

He stared out across a paved patio area leading away from open French doors providing a panoramic view of the Monaco coastline. Sipping jasmine tea from a bone china cup, he contemplated the azure blue waters a moment longer before turning back to the room, a frown creasing his features.

'You're absolutely sure about this, Sophie?'

'Without a doubt.' A slender woman with jet black hair sat on the white leather sofa beneath a gilt-framed mirror and crossed her legs, her grey trouser suit pristine. She held out a tablet computer to him, the silver bangles she wore on her left arm jangling. 'Photographic evidence, as requested.'

Elliott ignored it, wrinkled his nose and placed his cup and saucer on a desk carved from a single tree, the whorls and knots polished to a high sheen that reflected the spotlights in the high ceiling.

'Where was this taken?'

'North of Ankara – somewhere remote where the detonations wouldn't cause too much interest, apart from the local herdsmen. We were able to infiltrate the intelligence Ogilvy's contact received and draw them both out there. Both confirmed dead.'

'Has Dukes' body been recovered for identification?'

'Last night.' Sophie turned around the screen, then flicked through the images. 'Well, what was left of it anyway. There were two other people travelling in the vehicle with him at the time of impact.'

'Do we know who they were?'

'Not yet. Probably his local fixers, that's all.'

'Find out, Sophie. No loose ends, remember?'

'I understand.' She rose from the sofa and smoothed down her thin jacket. 'Was that all for now?'

'Yes. Send in Aaron, will you? And tell Sean I want to see him, too.'

Elliott reached out for a sheaf of financial statements that lay within an open leather signature folder and wandered out to the patio, his bare feet burning on the hot pavers before he reached the other side and descended onto the cool grass.

Palm trees swayed above a pagoda several metres away from the house, providing both shade and solitude from the main building.

After reclining in one of four wicker chairs and rearranging a cushion against his spine, Elliott pulled reading glasses from his shirt pocket, ran his thumb down the side of the page and smiled.

'Good news, I take it?'

A shadow fell across him, and he looked up, shading his eyes with his hand. 'Have a seat, Aaron. I presume your trip was successful?'

'As much as it could be in the circumstances, yes.' At forty-two, Aaron was three years his junior and the exact opposite in looks.

Whereas Elliott's complexion was pale and prone to sunburn, his brother's skin bore a perpetual tan all year round, enabling him to blend in more easily in a number of the countries within which they operated their burgeoning business.

Elliott leaned forward, placed the paperwork on a low table between the chairs and dropped a silver drinks coaster on the top to stop the pages fluttering away in the light breeze. That done, he removed his glasses and peered at his brother.

'Are you sure none of this can be traced back to us?'

'I'm sure.' Aaron sat, stretching out his long legs. 'As far as the embassy is concerned, the story is buried, along with Jeffrey Dukes. They haven't got a clue how it happened or who was responsible, so while they try to fathom out that – which they won't – they're going to lie about it.'

'But they'll keep digging.'

Aaron shrugged. 'Of course they will.'

'Are they going to find anything?'

'No.' Aaron's gaze locked with his for a moment, and then he choked out a laugh. 'Come on, Elliott. Relax.'

'I will, when this is done.'

He held up a hand as a younger man appeared at the side of the substantial property, lumbering towards them along a gravel path snaking around ornate grasses and exotic shrubs.

The man slowed as he grew nearer as if wary of the two men under the palm trees, and Elliott waved him forward with an exasperated sigh.

'I haven't got all day, Sean.' Elliott waited until Sean had walked over to where they sat, and then reached into his jacket pocket and unfolded an A4-sized piece of paper, flattening the creases with his hand before holding it up. 'Your ability to create problems continues, it seems. You were photographed at the airport on your arrival in Belarus. You're all over social media.'

The man paled, his gaze darting from Elliott to Aaron as he licked his lips. 'That's impossible. I took the usual precautions.'

'You were sloppy.' Elliott snapped, and jabbed his finger at the page. 'If you'd been taking precautions, you wouldn't have appeared in the background to this family's group photograph, would you?'

Sean's eyes fell to the image, and his Adam's apple bobbed. 'I– I don't know how that happened.'

Aaron emitted a snort, then looked away as Elliott glared at him before turning his attention back to the younger man.

'Why did you eliminate the Reaper crew? That wasn't in the plan.'

'One of them – the intel coordinator – recognised Dukes, I think.'

'What?' Elliott sat forward, unable to keep the shock from his voice. 'How?'

'I don't know. It was in the final seconds before the missile hit. She was about to change the camera angle when he peered out through the window of the vehicle. She got a clear view of him.'

'That doesn't explain why you killed the crew,' said Aaron.

'She started asking questions, all right?' Sean held up his hands. 'Look, maybe I panicked but I told her that her job was to follow orders, not ask questions. She stormed out of the command centre. Next thing I know, one of the men tells me that all three of them are making a run for it.'

'You panicked.' Elliott failed to keep the sneer from his voice.

'I didn't know what else to do!' The man looked from him to Aaron. 'Can't you see that if I'd let them go, they'd have found out we weren't who we said we were?'

'*You*, Sean – not we.' Elliott folded his hands in his lap. 'We have a further problem. One of the crew managed to escape.'

'I know. I'm sorry – I've got people trying to trace her.'

Elliott choked out a bitter laugh. 'You're too late – she's had help. Some sort of splinter group in Prague.'

Sean's brow furrowed before he turned to Aaron. 'We have people there. Send them after her.'

'We did. They're dead.'

'All of them?'

'All of them.'

Sean dropped his hands, his gaze falling to the lush grass. 'I'm sorry, Elliott. It won't happen again.'

'Your mistakes will make our work more difficult.' Elliott drummed his fingers on the arm of the wicker chair, then turned to his brother. 'Are you still walking around with that pistol you were showing me this morning?'

'Here.' Aaron opened his jacket and pulled the weapon from its holster before passing it to him.

'Thanks.'

Elliott swung around, aimed the weapon at Sean, and pulled the trigger before the man had a chance to react.

He fell to the ground as the gunshot echoed through the garden, his gaze a mixture of surprise and fright as he clutched at his chest, pawing at the blood oozing out from a gaping wound.

'You're right – it's balanced perfectly.' Elliott turned to Aaron and handed him the gun. 'Tell your contact we'll take fifty of them.'

'What are we going to do about the Hellfire missiles? We need more – and soon. We shouldn't have used the ones we had until we were assured of the next delivery.'

'We didn't have a choice. Our client insisted on a demonstration once he learned the command centre is constructed from parts sourced from several suppliers.' Elliott reached out and squeezed his shoulder. 'Don't worry. I have a source that I'm currently negotiating with in an attempt to secure a new delivery within the next three days. We'll arrange to take what we need before it reaches İzmir.'

'That's risky – they know about the other four now.'

'We don't have a choice. This deal will make us richer than we can imagine, and serve a higher purpose.'

'Are the finances in place?' Aaron jerked his chin towards the statements on the table. 'Everything good there?'

'Our buyer received approval for the money late last week. He's simply waiting for the funds to be transferred into his account so he can pay us. His superiors have no idea.'

'I take it the latest demonstration helped to sway him, then.'

'Just as well, given that he had to find his own crew.' Elliott extracted a piece of paper from his trouser pocket. 'In the meantime, it seems our friend Jeffrey Dukes had been up to his old tricks. He managed to post something to his girlfriend in London before he left Gaziantep for his final mission.'

'That was lucky.' Aaron's smile didn't reach his eyes. 'I'd best pay her a visit.'

'I'd expect no less.' Elliott stood and waved a dismissive hand at Sean's body, his lip curling as flies began to gather around the dead man. 'Deal with this mess before you leave.'

CHAPTER THIRTY-THREE

London

'Morning, Char – ready to do battle?'

Charlotte scowled into her coffee at the sound of Neil Hodges' voice carrying across the office to where she sat, then fixed a bright smile and turned as he drew closer.

'All set,' she said, handing him a manila folder and a printout of that morning's agenda.

'Good-o.' He placed his briefcase on the carpet and cleared his throat. 'Toskins in yet?'

'On his way.' She reached out and pointed to the diary entries in his hand. 'The meeting with the PM was brought forward to seven o'clock this morning, and your briefing with the Minister has been postponed until three this afternoon.'

'Oh, bollocks.' His face fell. 'I was hoping to follow up with him about our chat with Robert Nivens last night. Wonder why he didn't ask me to attend the meeting with the PM?'

Charlotte bit back the first retort that entered her head, and instead pasted a sympathetic smile to her lips. 'No idea, I'm afraid. I think it was very last-minute, Neil. Nothing personal.'

His jaw tightened. 'Even so, Char…'

Hodges picked up his briefcase and wandered across to his desk as his phone began to ring, and she turned back to her computer screen.

Opening a window beside the spreadsheet she was compiling, she ran her gaze over the headlines, but saw nothing new from last night's reports.

Jeffrey's death had already dropped below other stories, relegated to a minor headline several fonts smaller in size from the main reports now demanding the reader's attention.

She let out a shaking sigh, then closed the news site.

Everyone else in the office was talking about his health, the office gossips wondering aloud whether anyone had known he'd had heart complaints in the past, or if he had made any mention of health issues in passing.

There was no-one she could ask about the

documents he had sent to her prior to his death, not yet. Part of her ached to find out if he had sent anything else, to someone else.

Had he split up his research in an attempt to keep his knowledge safe?

And why had Hodges and Toskins been summoned to the Foreign Secretary's office late last night without anything appearing in their diaries?

She bit her lip.

What were the two men trying to hide?

Was it something to do with Jeffrey?

Hodges finished his call and wandered back to her. 'Everything all right, Char? You seem a bit quiet this morning.'

'Fine, Neil.' She saved the spreadsheet, then closed the screen and returned to her emails. 'Was there anything urgent you needed doing this morning?'

'I suppose not. Not now, anyway.'

He sighed, brow furrowing.

Charlotte shrugged – the man had a way of milking sympathy for the slightest reason and she wasn't in the mood to react to his insecurities.

'Great, well then I'm going to head upstairs,' she said, placing her bag in her desk drawer and locking it. 'I've got an admin meeting to attend.'

Picking up her mobile phone, she hurried from the office and into the corridor teeming with civil servants and hangers-on and crossed to one of the floor-to-ceiling windows overlooking Whitehall Place.

A steady drizzle peppered the glass as a diplomatic car dislodged a pair of men in dark suits onto the street, the driver pulling away from the kerb as soon as they had been greeted by a Whitehall Place acolyte armed with a large umbrella.

As they hurried under the portico to the building, Charlotte turned away and thumbed through her recent calls list.

She bit her lip.

Something wasn't right.

She could sense it.

Emails next. A quick scroll through the new messages provided no new information and she was reluctant to put anything in writing about Jeffrey's unscheduled trip to the Turkish-Syrian border.

Who were the three men he had described in his notes?

Were they British, or local people who had provided him with help during his time in Turkey?

As for Toskins' summons to the Prime Minister's office that morning, why so early?

The PM had a reputation for keeping long hours but there had been no announcements since.

Nothing to suggest there was anything wrong.

Her thumb hovered over an email she'd been copied into from the Foreign Office – Jeffrey's department. It was dated two weeks ago from Robert Nivens, the Foreign Secretary himself.

The message was short, to the point, and requested that Toskins provide a copy of a recent agreement that he had struck with the leader of a small country on the fringes of sub-Saharan Africa. Nivens had been approached by a human rights organisation raising concerns about the deal, citing fears that the weapons sold by the British government would be used against civil rights campaigners protesting the current incumbent's policies and past atrocities.

The request had caused some consternation within the Department for International Trade, and Charlotte recalled the heated argument between Toskins and Hodges before the door to the Minister's office had flown open and Hodges stalked past her desk without a backward glance, his jaw clenched.

Nothing more had been said since, and she hadn't been copied into any further correspondence in the matter.

Charlotte glanced up at the sound of Toskins' name, a wave of guilt sweeping through her.

She relaxed a little when she saw the two men she'd seen getting out of the car conversing beneath a framed photograph of the Palace of Westminster, their expressions harried.

Resigning herself to the knowledge that she wouldn't be able to find out more about Jeffrey and his supposed health issues by reading tabloid news apps or departmental emails, she flicked the screen to sleep and wandered over.

'Can I help you, gentlemen? I'm with the Minister's office.'

The older man gave a tight smile. 'Gerald Knox. We've got an urgent appointment with the Minister about Jeffrey Dukes.'

CHAPTER THIRTY-FOUR

Miles swiped his security pass before lowering his face to a retinal scanner beside the reinforced steel door, and tried to batten down the rising panic in his chest.

Since Knox had returned from his meeting with Edward Toskins and reported that the Minister was unable to shed any light on the stolen missiles – or confirm whether the theft was a one-off or simply the latest in a string of similar raids on arms shipments – the whole Section had mobilised in an effort to trace what else might have been taken.

And find out where it was going.

The door lock clicked, and Miles pushed his way into a box-like chamber whereupon he placed his mobile phone, car key fob and wallet into a numbered locker. He swiped his pass across a panel below the locker and it swung shut.

He would retrieve his belongings upon leaving the central operations room, not before.

Turning to a set of glass doors, he paused while they swished open and then walked into a darkened room with no windows.

The only light source came from tiny spotlights in the ceiling and from the glow of the computer monitors his small team sat in front of.

Miles paced the ops centre floor, crossing to the wall beyond the desks, and stood in front of a bank of screens displaying composite images from different satellites across Eastern Europe.

His three key analysts worked with their heads bowed as they typed new commands into their computers, the images on the screens flickering and changing in real-time as new information was downloaded and processed in seconds.

A database calculated complex algorithms, cross-referenced places and names and intercepted phone calls and encrypted messages from Section agents on the ground, all of whom were deciphering reports of potential sightings or discarding information designed to confuse and delay the hunt for the missing drone command centre.

Miles turned to face his colleagues and ran his eyes over the discarded coffee cups and takeaway cartons littering the desks beside them.

They had been working non-stop now for over

twelve hours, but wouldn't take a break – not until they found their target.

He wandered over to a spare desk beside them and sank into a chair with a sigh.

'Okay, so we can't access satellite data or intercepted communications on mobile networks without alerting MI6 and GCHQ thanks to the Prime Minister's instructions to Knox, so what are we left with?'

'We've got access to local police and military databases throughout Eastern Europe,' said Jason. 'We also have access to their communications, along with mobile phone comms and CCTV cameras in major residential areas. Basically, everything we would normally get from our colleagues, except we can't.'

'Okay, let's start in Belarus,' said Miles. 'We know from the information that Marie has given us what the approximate dimensions of the command centre are. What else?'

'That's been confirmed with the information that we've acquired from RAF Waddington,' said Greg. 'They've given us a good idea of what to look for because it's often how they transport their own command centres.'

'Have we got anything to get us started?'

Jason tapped his screen. 'We have. Again Marie was able to identify the airfield they flew from when she was with Eva and Nathan. From there, we've got movement twenty-four hours ago.'

'Anything since?'

A silence descended while the analysts returned to their screens, and Miles slapped his hand on the desk.

'Anybody? Any ideas? Where has it gone?' said Miles. 'Come on, this is urgent. They may well be re-arming in the next two days if we can't confirm which shipment of arms is their next target. If they killed two people, they did it for a reason and they're not going to stop now.'

'I think I've got something,' Emily said. She tapped the screen in front of her, then hit a button and the panels on the wall flickered and changed once more. 'Here.'

Miles watched as the satellite's powerful lens zoomed in to a small town west of Minsk in Belarus. 'Where is this?'

'This footage is from CCTV cameras in Kobryn. It's on the border with Poland,' she said, using her mouse to draw a circle around a narrow road leading between the two countries. 'It stood out for me because it's off the main route away from the highways that you'd normally see intercontinental freight using.'

Pushing back his chair as she started the playback on the recording, he watched as a truck slowed to negotiate a crossroads, its brake lights flaring.

Moments later, it roared out the other side of the

small town and into the darkness beyond the last CCTV camera.

'When was this?'

'Half past eleven last night.'

A pale coloured shipping container was on the trailer the truck towed, its surface displaying the name of a food company.

'Have you traced this company name?' said Miles.

'It doesn't exist,' said Emily. 'There isn't a single company registered in Europe with that name.'

'What if he's just someone moving house?' said Greg, turning his pen between his fingers.

'He didn't stop at any of the usual truck stops,' said Emily. 'He's been stopping to refuel. I've traced his route since he left Poland. And he's keeping to himself. He's refuelling at small town petrol stations and going out of his way to avoid other drivers. This is a screen capture from the last time he refilled – it's at Târgoviște in Romania. I've already contacted one of our in-country agents and she confirms that he paid cash. I've lost sight of him since then.'

Jason sighed. 'So we haven't even got financial data to trace who he is.'

'Emily, zoom out from that view, and let's have a look at potential routes beyond Târgoviște to known risk areas. Include everything on our watch lists,' said Miles, rolling up his shirt sleeves. 'Greg – run the data on historical intercepts from the last three months. That way, the other intelligence services will think we're auditing the systems or doing a purge of data from the databases as a housekeeping exercise.'

The analyst at the end of the row of desks raised an eyebrow. 'Do you think they'll fall for it?'

'Have you got a better suggestion?'

'Onto it.'

Miles pushed back his chair and bit back his frustration.

His team were tired, working as fast as they could, and were among some of the best data analysts in the country.

And yet the clock was ticking, and if the plan Knox was devising failed, then the drone and its last remaining Hellfire missile could be used anywhere, against anyone.

The consequences could be catastrophic.

'Miles – take a look at this.'

He turned at Greg's voice. 'Have you found it?'

In response, Greg pointed at the bank of screens as a new image blinked onto the wall in front of him.

'No, but this is a report that's just come in from the fire department in Atârnati, north of Bucharest. They're responding to a call from a resident about a truck that's on fire under a concrete bridge beneath the main highway.'

'Can you translate it?'

'I can do better – I'm patching into a camera on top of a nearby radio station. Here we go.'

Miles rested a hand on top of Greg's computer screen as he peered at the grainy image, at the smoke billowing from an off-white shipping container atop a trailer.

The truck's cab was consumed by flames quickly spreading along the length of the trailer, and as he narrowed his eyes he could make out a gaping hole in the side of the shipping container.

'Fuck,' he managed eventually.

'What do you want us to do, Miles?' said Emily.

He drummed his fingers on the top of the monitor for a moment longer, and then snatched up his security pass and ran for the glass doors.

'I think I'd better tell Knox.'

CHAPTER THIRTY-FIVE

Slovakia

Eva placed another log on the fire, closing the cast iron door as a spark popped and hit the glass.

'That got cold fast,' said Nathan as she joined him on the sofa and handed her bottle of beer.

'It will for another couple of weeks,' said Decker. The older assassin sat on the floor with his back to the other sofa as he gazed into the fire's glow. 'Best time of year to visit if you need to relax.'

Eva couldn't disagree with him as she cast her gaze out through the windows while the sun began to set – the journey out of Belarus and through the southern edge of Poland had been fraught with tension and disagreements.

Sitting on a concrete plinth on the edge of one of the burned-out aircraft hangars, Nathan had logged into an encrypted server and contacted the Section, suggesting he and Eva make their way to Poland while awaiting further orders.

Decker had been keen as well, arguing that they were on hand and available.

Knox was having none of it.

'You're all persona non grata in Poland after your last mission,' he growled. 'You cross the border, and we might not be able to get you back. It's bad enough you chose to cut through there to get to Belarus.'

After that, they received an encrypted message from Miles with instructions to head south west to Slovakia instead and to wait for further orders once they were there.

The guesthouse on the fringes of Brastilava had been a welcome sight, given both its proximity to several roads leading away from the city, and its position.

Set back from the road along a winding path leading to lovingly tended gardens and a lake, the location provided ample views in all directions – perfect for maintaining a lookout for any unwanted attention or threats.

Eva turned away from the view and wandered over to the sofa.

'How did you know about this place, Decker?' she said, as Nathan worked at his laptop. 'Friend of yours?'

'From way back.'

'Handy.' She took a sip of beer. 'All right – what are your thoughts on why we're here, and why Knox didn't want us to go after the command centre?'

Nathan's fingers paused above the keyboard. 'Like Knox said – we're still wanted in Poland.'

Decker chuckled. 'Hasn't stopped him sending us places before, has it?'

'True,' said Eva. 'What do you think, then?'

'I reckon the shit's hit the fan.' Decker wiped the back of his hand across his mouth and placed his empty beer bottle on the stone hearth.

'What makes you say that?' said Nathan.

'The way the order came to leave the airfield, and the radio silence since. Something's got them spooked.'

Eva checked her watch. 'What time were they supposed to call us?'

'Five minutes ago,' said Nathan. He frowned at his laptop screen. 'Plenty of signal here, and the encryption programme's working fine...'

Eva yawned, the effect of a Slovakian stew followed by plum rolls and then relaxing in front of a fire proving too much. 'I can't believe how much food we just ate.'

Decker grinned. 'Wait until you see breakfast.'

She groaned, then sat upright as Nathan's laptop emitted a high-pitched *ping*.

'Here we go.' He crossed the living area to a square dining table in the corner away from the window and began talking before he'd settled on one of the chairs. 'Everything all right?'

'I'll explain in a minute,' replied Miles. 'Everyone else there?'

Eva pulled out a chair next to Nathan and waited for Decker to join them, although he took the chair behind the laptop screen to avoid being seen, then leaned forward and folded her arms.

'Did Marie get to you safely?'

'She did,' said Knox, coming into view and sipping from a water glass. 'We've got her here at headquarters in one of the guest suites. She'll start helping us with the investigation from our end in the morning once she's had a chance to rest.'

'Thanks,' said Nathan.

'Any news on where that command centre is now?' said Eva.

'We've had some new intel come through in the past hour,' said Miles. 'The shipping container is in Atârnati, a town north of Bucharest.'

Eva groaned when he told them about the burned-out truck. 'Same as the hangars at the airfield.'

'Except they stripped all the equipment out the back of the container first. That's still missing.'

'What about the driver?' said Eva. 'Any sign of him?'

'What was left of him was in the container,' said Knox. 'Looks like they threw acid over his hands and face first to make absolutely sure he couldn't be identified.'

'Hang on,' said Nathan. 'If they were planning on heading to Romania, why didn't they drive straight through the Ukraine?'

'Perhaps trying to avoid detection.' Decker folded his arms over his chest and raised an eyebrow.

'That's what we're thinking,' said Miles. 'The place is still under a lot of surveillance from NATO and the NSA, though of course they won't confirm that.'

'Whoever stripped out the shipping container can easily find another one to retrofit with the equipment necessary to fly that drone,' said Nathan. 'It's easier to transport it undetected if it's broken up into smaller parts, isn't it?'

'So, where's the command centre heading?' said Eva. 'What's its final destination? Romania, or somewhere else?'

'I've been having some discreet discussions with the Foreign Secretary and Edward Toskins about that.' Knox leaned forward, his eyes troubled. 'Given the direction of travel and the current ambitions of some members of the government, we believe the equipment for the command centre is being transported through Bulgaria to northern Turkey. We haven't located the drone yet – it could be there already.'

'Why Turkey?'

'Because any instability there would impact both Europe and the Middle East,' said Miles. 'We've been taking another look at reports coming in over the past six months and we think whoever's behind all of this is trying to take advantage of that. Jeffrey Dukes was active in Ankara before his death, and we have to assume he got too close to the truth.'

'Shit,' said Decker. 'That changes things. When do we leave?'

The Section chief wagged his finger at them. 'I don't want you heading there just yet.'

'Why the hell not?'

'There's a more pressing matter,' said Miles.

'I doubt it.'

Knox glared at Decker's response, and Eva shook her head at the older assassin before turning back to the screen.

'What is it?'

'A second attack was made prior to the airfield in Belarus being abandoned,' said the Section chief.

'Where?' Eva asked.

'A hundred miles or so north of Ankara.' The screen changed to show an image of a man wearing a business suit and smiling at the camera in a posed photograph that looked as if it was from a company website. 'Do either of you recognise this man?'

Nathan shook his head.

'Never seen him before in my life,' said Eva.

'We've had word come in that the director of an NGO based in Ankara left his hotel yesterday and didn't return,' said Knox. 'Goes by the name of Adrian Ogilvy. His room had been ransacked. There were no fingerprints – whoever did it was a professional, and we can't be certain what they were looking for. The remains of his vehicle and one belonging to a local man called Mahdi were found destroyed out in the middle of nowhere.'

'That doesn't mean it was a drone strike,' said Decker.

Miles flicked up a satellite image. 'It does when there are two fucking great craters like this.'

'Shit.'

'Three strikes, three missiles,' said Eva. 'Whoever this is, they've got one left.'

'Which means they're either saving the last one for a specified target, or—'

'—they're waiting for supplies,' said Decker.

'How do you know he was killed with the same drone?' said Nathan.

'We don't, not for sure but given the fact that both his vehicle and that of a local man were found at the site of two reported explosions out in the desert, and that the damage sustained to those vehicles and the immediate landscape is not dissimilar to that seen in missile attacks, we have to conclude that Ogilvy was targeted by the same person or people who killed Jeffrey Dukes.'

'Why target either of those? What connects them?'

'We'll get to that in a moment,' said Knox. 'The point is—'

'Whoever's behind this is almost out of ammunition,' said Decker. 'He's got one missile left, so he'll need more for whatever he's got planned now that the shipment to restock the drone was intercepted.'

'Working on the basis our enemy will try to infiltrate another legitimate shipment of arms, we met with Edward Toskins from the Department for International Trade this morning,' said Miles. 'He's given us a list of recent arms sales the British government has approved and there's only one that includes Hellfire missiles. That left Florida yesterday afternoon.'

'What's the likelihood of those missiles being intercepted en route?' said Eva.

'None, not now,' said Knox. 'We shared our intel with our counterparts in the US and there are now agents on that ship, and a submarine escort. They'll also work with MI6 to make sure agents are at the ports the ship intends to visit prior to getting to İzmir.'

'That's something, at least,' said Nathan, 'but what connects Ogilvy to the Foreign Office – let alone Dukes?'

'We've found out who Jeffrey Dukes really was.' Miles picked up a document and scanned the page before his gaze returned to the screen. 'Both men were members of the Association of Former Intelligence Officers.'

'Told you – spooks,' said Decker, unable to keep the smug tone from his voice. 'It's always bloody spooks.'

Eva ignored him. 'What's their history?'

'Ogilvy used to work in West Berlin for Interpol back in the late eighties, and Dukes was active for MI6 – they won't tell us where, but we're presuming he was working behind the Iron Curtain for a period of time.' Miles put the document to one side. 'At least that explains why we couldn't find a history for him – not a believable one – beyond his time at the Foreign Office, anyway.'

'I've never heard of the Association,' said Nathan, his fingers working the keyboard to bring up an encrypted search engine.

'It's US-based with a few international members,' said Knox. 'It's not secretive in any way – they share open information, discuss bilateral agreements, organise get-togethers during the year—'

'Why kill two retired spies in such a way?' Eva shoved back her chair and paced the floor. 'What was the point?'

'We think we might be able to shed some light on that,' said Knox. 'When we met with Toskins earlier, he confirmed that Dukes was due to meet with Ogilvy while in Ankara last week. Obviously, Toskins was under the impression it was to do with some sort of trade deal, but when we spoke to MI6 and dug a little deeper, it turns out Dukes knew Ogilvy from the old days. They used to trade information – what we're trying to do is find out whether they were still doing so, and why.'

'Whatever it was, it's evident they got too close and whoever's behind this decided to stop them. Permanently,' said Miles. 'I've got a team of analysts trying to trace where that command centre's been moved to. I've still got contacts in the NSA so we might be able to piggy-back off of one of their satellites.'

'We've also spoken to the Association of Former Intelligence Officers in the US and asked them for a list of British members,' said Knox. There's only one left now. Patrick Leavey.'

'Where's he?' said Eva.

'Lisbon,' said Miles. 'There's an address for him on file, but it's several years old.'

Knox cleared his throat. 'Your mission is to go to Portugal, find Patrick Leavey, and then get him to North Africa.'

'Why North Africa?' said Nathan.

'Because the ship is due to dock in Algiers before heading for Malta and İzmir,' said Knox, 'and there's plenty of open desert around that destination. If we can convince whoever's in charge of that drone that Patrick has discovered what their plans are and that he's there to stop them, we might be able to force their hand.'

Eva narrowed her eyes. 'Are you saying you want to use Leavey to draw out this rogue Reaper – as bait – in order to use up its last missile before they can resupply or find out about the intercept planned in Malta?'

'Exactly.'

'Fuck me,' said Decker, a look of disbelief crossing his chiselled features. 'He's not going to like that, is he?'

CHAPTER THIRTY-SIX

Lisbon, Portugal

Eva pulled her sunglasses off her head, swung her backpack over her shoulder and fell into step beside Decker and Nathan.

The Sete Rios bus station hummed with activity, heaving with a swarming mass of people departing vehicles that had travelled several hundred miles across Europe before ending their journey at the coastal city.

She glared at a youth who eyed her hungrily, his gaze lingering over her as if weighing up what valuables she might be carrying, and then flicked back her jacket to reveal the gun tucked into her waistband.

His eyes widened, the cigarette dangling from his lips falling to the pavement before he scurried away.

'Stop that,' said Decker. 'There are cameras coming up.'

Eva grinned, and adjusted her jacket.

'The trams are this way.' Nathan jerked his head towards a sign, then peered at his phone screen. 'We can catch one into the centre and then walk from there.'

'Why can't we walk from here?' said Decker. 'Less chance of being seen.'

'Because if the past few days are anything to go by, we might already be too late,' said Eva under her breath. 'If Knox and Miles are right about these men, then Patrick Leavey is a target too. It's been bad enough having to travel by bus to avoid the airports. We've lost a day and a half already.'

'I still don't like it.'

'Tough.'

Twenty minutes later, they disembarked beside a busy square lined with restaurants and cafés teeming with tourists, and slunk into the shadows of a side street out of sight.

'It's a quarter mile from here to Leavey's last known address,' said Nathan, holding up his phone to improve the signal. 'Follow me.'

'Don't lead us right to him,' warned Eva. 'Give me a heads up when we're a few hundred metres away, all right?'

The former intelligence officer gave Eva a quick

smile, then led them on a snaking route leading away from the square and into Bairro Alto.

Eva cast her gaze over graffiti-tagged walls, admiring the intricate designs and artwork in between the childish tags peppering the brickwork.

The narrow lanes held a desolation borne of an area used to waking at night and sleeping during the day.

Shirts, blouses and other items of clothing flapped from washing lines strung across wrought-iron balconies, the colours a striking contrast to the grey security shutters protecting the nightclubs and bars from unwanted attention.

A radio played through one of the open windows, its volume kept low as the soft music wafted over their heads, the dulcet tones of a classical guitar thrumming beneath the chirping from caged birds who peered with beady eyes from their lofty perches.

Eva turned her attention to a narrow street that ended on her left, a steep incline arcing away from their position.

A yellow and white tram stood stationary on its funicular rails, the driver mumbling to another man who crouched next to the rear bogey wheels and muttered a response as he whacked the axle of the vintage streetcar with a large spanner before shaking his head.

'It's up here.'

Nathan's voice roused her from her observations,

and she turned her attention to see him waiting patiently at a crossroads.

He indicated to a building a hundred metres away on their right, its peeling honey-coloured façade in shadow.

The small group crossed the street, hugging the plasterwork walls of the neighbouring properties before slipping into a stone-hewn alcove.

A wooden green door blocked their entry, and Eva ran her finger down the list of names beside a security panel set into the stone wall.

'Which apartment?' she hissed.

'Three,' said Nathan.

She hit the button for apartment five, a soft buzz filling the air.

'*Olá.*'

'*Entrega,*' Eva replied, and crossed her fingers.

'What are you going to do if someone comes down the stairs looking for their delivery?' said Decker.

She shrugged as the door gave under her touch and she pushed it open. 'Tell them I got the wrong address.'

A coolness enveloped her as she stepped into the hallway, the polished stone tiles deadening her footsteps. She turned as Decker and Nathan joined her, the latter easing the door closed.

Resting her hand on the wooden balustrade, she peered through the railings up to the first landing.

Two doors faced the stairs, both closed and both in need of new paint.

From behind the one on the right she could hear a radio playing – a rock anthem she recognised from her teens. From the other—

Nothing.

'I can't hear a fucking thing over that music,' she hissed to Decker.

'If Leavey's in there, then neither will he,' came the reply.

The older assassin began walking up the stairs without waiting for her response, and she glanced over her shoulder at Nathan.

'Do we follow?' he said.

Eva shook her head.

No sense in all of them getting shot if Leavey took exception to the interruption to his daily routine.

Movement to her right sent goosebumps flittering across her forearms and she turned to see the apartment door beside them open a crack.

An old woman peered out, grey hair escaping from under a brightly-coloured scarf and keen grey eyes behind a pair of glasses. She wore a bright yellow housecoat over jeans and held a cigarette between her lips.

'Who are you?' she said, her voice no more than a rasp. 'What do you want?'

Eva waved her back. 'We're looking for a friend of ours. Nothing to worry about.'

The woman frowned, removed the cigarette, then

pointed upwards with it. 'Above here? The Englishman?'

'Yes.'

'He is not in.'

'Are you sure?'

'I watch everyone.'

Eva grinned. 'I'm sure you do. Do you know where he went?'

'No.'

'Any idea when he might be back?'

'No.'

Eva turned away from her as Decker appeared at the top of the stairs.

'The apartment's deserted,' he said in a low tone. 'Looks like he cleared out a while back. There's nothing there.'

The old woman crushed the cigarette under her shoe as she stepped into the hallway and pushed Eva to one side before peering up the stairs. 'Decker?'

He frowned. 'How the hell do you know my name?'

In response, she pulled Eva across the threshold, beckoning to the others.

'Get inside, now,' she hissed.

CHAPTER THIRTY-SEVEN

Recovering from the initial shock, Eva twisted in the woman's grip as she tumbled over the threshold and slammed her into the wall beside the door.

She wrenched the woman's arm behind her back as Nathan and Decker stormed into the room, surprised at the strength and resistance she met.

The older assassin closed the door and forced his face next to the woman's as she tried to lift her cheek from the plasterwork.

'Start talking.'

'I will. Let me go. I'm not your enemy.'

Decker gave a quick nod to Eva and she stepped away, confident that with three of them against one, the woman posed no further threat.

The woman exhaled, rubbing her wrist.

'Thank you.'

Eva watched, fascinated as the woman moved to lock the door then straightened, gaining another two inches in height before whipping the scarf from her head and removing a grey wig.

Next, she began to tear at her skin, picking away at the flesh until it came away in strips that she balled into her fist.

'Latex,' she mumbled, except her voice was deeper now, baritone.

She took off her glasses before removing coloured contact lenses, then grinned and stuck fingers into her mouth and removed padding from her cheeks.

The effect was complete.

Instead of an old wizened woman, a man in his early sixties stood before them, green eyes keen as he registered their surprised faces while he exchanged his housecoat for a white cotton shirt that he tucked into his jeans.

'Patrick Leavey?' said Decker.

'Yes.'

'How do you know who I am?'

Eva placed her hand on the assassin's arm, confusion radiating off him as he glared at the former agent. 'He has a point, Leavey.'

'All in good time.' Leavey crossed a threadbare rug to the shuttered windows and opened the wooden blinds a crack. 'Did anyone follow you here?'

'No – we doubled back a few times on the way here,' said Eva. 'We haven't been traced.'

'Yet.' Leavey sighed and turned back to them. 'Who do you work for, then?'

'The Section.'

'Knox's black ops project?' His eyes widened. 'I thought that got mothballed years ago.'

'You wish,' Decker sneered. 'You still haven't answered my question. What are you? Ex-MI6?'

'A long time ago.' Leavey paused, pulled a cigarette packet from his back pocket and lit one before blowing smoke up to the ceiling. 'I came across your skills in Belgium, late '99. The target was a Hungarian dissident hoping to sell his secrets to the West while on a trade mission. You were sent to dispatch him after we discovered he was a double agent working for the KGB.' He shrugged, his face rueful. 'There are some jobs where MI6 prefers to keep a hands-off approach, more's the pity.'

Decker's lip curled. 'I remember the job. I don't remember you.'

'I was the one who was sent in to clean up afterwards. I recognised you from the surveillance footage we were watching during the op. We were parked half a mile away.'

'What do you want, an apology?'

Leavey chuckled. 'No. We were both simply doing our jobs back then, weren't we?'

Eva held out her hand and made the introductions.

'Yes,' said Leavey. 'I've heard your names before, too. Why are you here?'

'First of all, why the subterfuge with the dressing up?' said Nathan. 'Have you received threats?'

'Oh, all the time.' Leavey waved them across to a round wooden table at the back of the room while he threw the cosmetic aids into a rubbish bin beside a single stove. After placing the glasses, wig and scarf on the worktop, he turned to them. He gave an apologetic shrug, although a smile creased his features. 'Can't take any chances at the moment.'

'Tell us about Jeffrey Dukes and Adrian Ogilvy,' said Decker.

Leavey's smile vanished. 'So, that's why you're here. It's true, then? They're both dead?'

'Murdered,' said Eva.

The former MI6 agent leaned against the workshop and lit another cigarette, his brow furrowed as she told him what had happened to his comrades. He shook his head when she finished, his green eyes troubled.

'I worried about Jeffrey after I heard nothing since receiving a message from him over a week ago. I didn't know about Adrian.'

'What did Jeffrey's message say?' said Nathan.

'That he believed he'd identified the person using the British government's arms trade agreements to smuggle arms to unapproved countries, and that those countries could pose a threat to the stability of the region.'

'Given their current policies of supplying finance and arms to suppressive regimes, that doesn't surprise me,' said Decker. 'What's so different about the countries being supplied on the black market?'

'We – myself, Adrian and Jeffrey – think someone is trying to break the stranglehold on oil and gas supplies in the Middle East. Rather than the West trying to dictate terms with OPEC, why not simply reset the whole region, disrupt supply at that end and then renegotiate who's entitled to what?'

'But the British government already supplies arms to countries in the Middle East,' said Eva. 'What difference will it make?'

'Because the man behind this isn't supporting those countries – if he did, nothing would change. No, our research shows that the illegal arms are being sold to a country on the fringes of the Middle East and Europe run by a man with ambition. The problem is, he doesn't know he's being used because his ego is clouding his judgement.'

'In what way?' said Decker. 'And by who?'

'Think about it – what if a war was started by the leader of a country who had no other interest but to reset that power balance so that he could then take advantage amongst all the confusion? And, what if he was supported by someone with a vested interest in the outcome? Someone who would make money from the ensuing war – and the aftermath?'

Eva leaned back in her chair, and drummed her fingers on the table. 'It's been done before.'

'Exactly. Often with the public being told that a despot needs to be removed,' said Leavey, his eyes gleaming. 'Except this time, a Western government isn't involved. It's one man.'

'You said you found out who,' she said.

The former MI6 agent nodded. 'It was only by chance. We used to catch up for drinks in London from time to time—'

'The Association of Former Intelligence Officers,' said Nathan.

'Yes.'

'So much for being retired,' said Decker.

Leavey's mouth twisted. 'I don't think you ever retire from this, do you? Anyway, both Adrian and Jeffrey were working legitimate jobs these past few years – I think they found other causes to get their teeth into, but they always kept their ears open. The skills might get rusty over time, but you never lose them completely.'

'Who's your target?' said Eva.

'Elliott Wilder.'

Nathan coughed. 'The owner of the biggest supplier of weapons to the British government?'

Leavey jabbed his cigarette towards him. 'That's the one.'

'Why? He's already making a shit ton of money through legitimate arms sales. Why do this?'

'Because Elliott Wilder is a Russian agent.'

CHAPTER THIRTY-EIGHT

'Mr Wilder?'

Elliott flicked down the top of the broadsheet newspaper he was reading and peered over it as a slim woman in her mid-forties approached the cluster of Chesterfield armchairs, a welcoming smile on her lips as she balanced a clutch of manila folders under one arm.

'Charlotte Hughes,' she said, extending a hand as he stood. 'We've spoken on the phone. If you'd like to come with me? He's ready to see you now.'

'Thank you.'

He leaned over, drained the last of his coffee, then picked up his briefcase and fell into step beside Charlotte as she led him away from the plush surroundings of the reception area and along a wide corridor.

'I trust you had a good flight?' she said, steering him

through a melee of junior civil servants who were talking at the top of their voices.

'I did, thank you.' He shot her a casual smile. 'The benefits of having one's own private aircraft.'

'Indeed,' she replied. 'City Airport, wasn't it?'

'Yes.'

She paused beside a wooden panelled door. 'Here we are.'

Charlotte knocked once, then opened it and stepped to one side to let him pass.

'Elliott – good to see you,' bellowed Edward Toskins.

The Minister for the Department for International Trade moved away from the large windows overlooking Whitehall Place and rounded the large conference table, beaming.

'Edward, likewise – I was surprised to get your call, though.'

'Just a formality, old boy. Appreciate you coming all this way at short notice.' Toskins pumped his hand, his cheeks flushed with the signs of a man who enjoyed a brandy or three on a daily basis. He turned to the other man in the room. 'I don't believe you've met my senior adviser, Neil Hodges.'

Elliott nodded to Hodges, declining to shake his hand and instead turning his attention to Charlotte as she set out the manila folders alongside water glasses, notepaper embossed with the Ministry's letterhead, and complimentary pens.

The room held a mustiness, a history that soaked into the thick crimson carpet and oak-panelled walls, and he took a moment to savour the moment, conscious of the part he was about to play in the near future of the country's political wrangling.

'Take a seat, Elliott,' Toskins said, waving his hand expansively. 'Anywhere you like.'

Moving around to a seat by the window and facing the only door in and out of the room, Elliott busied himself with the contents of his briefcase while the others took their places.

'Char – could you chase up some tea and coffee?' said Hodges. 'That is, if Mr Wilder would like some?'

The woman grimaced at the familiarity but, to her credit, forced a smile.

'I'm fine, thank you. I'm sure Ms Hughes has enough to do,' said Elliot, 'but you go ahead if you need something.'

'No – no, that's all right,' Hodges simpered. 'As long as our guest is comfortable.'

Elliott dropped his gaze to avoid Charlotte's ill-disguised smirk, took his seat and folded his hands on top of the folder she had left in front of him.

Remaining silent while the two men traded chit-chat and attempted to convey a sense of business as usual while taking their seats opposite him, Elliott ran his eyes over the paperwork they laid out.

No surprises – as he and Aaron had suspected, the British government was covering up the theft of four Hellfire missiles, and was now busy interviewing suppliers to find out who to blame for the lax security that led to it.

He bit back a surprised retort at the second name on the list – he hadn't been aware that the Brits had awarded a contract to that company, and resolved to task Aaron with a little corporate espionage in the coming weeks to find out why they had been successful, and then systematically destroy their credibility.

'Now, Elliott. Sorry to be an absolute bore, but needs must,' said Toskins. 'This request comes straight from the top – the PM herself – and one of our intelligence agencies, so we have to be seen to be toeing the line.'

Elliott smiled. 'Not a problem, Edward. I'd expect nothing less from a man of your stature.'

The Minister visibly preened. 'Charlotte, dear – ready to take notes?'

'Yes, Minister.'

'Elliott, as you can see from the papers we have here, we had a situation in İzmir last week whereby a shipment of arms from the US was missing four Hellfire missiles,' said Toskins. 'Hate to bring this up, old chap, but we're concerned as to who knew about the missiles being on board in the first place. We're at a loss as to what went wrong. Perhaps you could tell us whether you've received any threats to your business or are aware of any problems in the past?'

'I'm very sorry to learn about this,' said Elliott. 'I can assure you that if this had been brought to my attention at the time, I would have been able to ascertain from my associates in the US whether there were any threats made,' he said, leaning back in his seat and savouring the late afternoon sunlight that bathed his shoulders. 'However, it would have been more prudent if you'd asked me when the theft was first discovered. As you know, I have innumerable people at my disposal who could help with any investigation.'

Toskins cleared his throat, and lowered his voice. 'Yes, well, I must apologise that no-one in my office thought to contact you last week.' He waved his hand at the woman. 'No need to note this, Charlotte. We only found out about it ourselves four days ago, and as you'll appreciate we deal with a number of arms suppliers so these meetings have been non-stop since.'

Elliott shot him an enigmatic smile as Charlotte picked up her pen once more. 'I understand from my sources that the ship conveying the container made two stops prior to arriving in İzmir. What efforts have been made to see if the missiles were stolen there?'

'Our intelligence agencies report they have nothing to share with us yet,' said Hughes, and wrinkled his nose. 'They tell us they're underfunded and understaffed.'

'Well, I do hope you'll let me know when they're concluded, and what you've managed to glean from your investigation,' said Elliott.

'Of course, of course,' Toskins glared at Hodges before turning back to Elliott, his cheeks flushing. 'So as far as you're aware, Elliott, those missiles were not removed by any of your subcontractors? Even by accident, shall we say?'

'I should hope not. My contractors have the highest security clearances,' he said, tapping the pages in front of him and injecting a note of consternation into his voice, 'unlike some of our smaller competitors, by the look of it.'

Toskins' face flushed. 'Well, good. Good. I'm very glad to hear it, Elliott – and thank you for being so frank with us.'

'Not a problem, Edward.' Elliott flashed a smile at the two men, then flicked his wrist and checked his watch. 'Are we done here? It's just that the Foreign Secretary's asked me to have drinks with him at five.'

CHAPTER THIRTY-NINE

Eva couldn't prevent the choked gasp that escaped her lips. 'What proof have you got that Elliott Wilder is a Russian agent?'

Patrick Leavey pulled out a chair and dropped into it with a sigh.

In that moment, she noticed the dark circles under his eyes and the weariness in his shoulders, and wondered what he had done for Queen and country over the decades.

As if sensing her concern, he managed a small smile before continuing.

'His parents moved to the UK from Romania in the 1960s – they were lucky to get out by all accounts, but the Russians kept an eye on them, particularly their son. We think the KGB got their claws into him at university in the late seventies.'

'Bloody hell,' said Decker. 'And no-one ever knew?'

'Too much else going on with nuclear Armageddon just around the corner in '83 thanks to the Able Archer NATO exercises,' said Leavey. 'After university, Wilder set up various companies, selling them at a profit each time until finally establishing the arms supply business he has now.'

'How'd he get away with that?' said Nathan.

Leavey shrugged. 'It's a legitimate business. He pays his taxes, supports a number of veterans' associations – ironic, I know – and he's friends with several government ministers. He's used the business to whittle his way into British government contracts. Using it as a front, he's now covertly selling arms to countries that will cause unrest – unrest that will play into the Russian government's wider plans to destabilise Europe and sour its relationship with the United States.'

'Why kill Dukes and Ogilvy?' said Eva. 'Did they get too close?'

'That, and the fact we're the only ones who can identify him,' said Leavey. 'Our individual agencies – MI6 and Interpol – had a watching brief on Elliott Wilder during the eighties and early nineties while he was building up his business empire. The agencies watched everyone that had a remote link with communism. He was too good for us, though. We never managed to get any proof to support the suspicions about him at the time, but the three of us kept an open file on him and a few others, just in case.'

'And being retired, you haven't had the full support of your old network to protect yourselves while you tried to uncover what he was up to, right?'

'Yes, and because the UK side of the Association is so fractured compared to that of our US compatriots, we didn't have such a strong network of people to call on. We knew we were dealing with a dangerous man. They both knew the risks.' Leavey shook his head. 'It doesn't make it any easier to bear, though. How did they die – have you got any intel about that?'

Eva told him, and saw the hatred in his expression as he clenched his fists.

'He'll pay for that,' he said. 'I don't know how, but I will make him pay.'

'How did he locate them so easily?' said Nathan. 'Our lot couldn't find any history for them prior to their current jobs – nothing legitimate once they started digging, anyway.'

'For someone like Elliott, it wouldn't have been difficult. Money talks, after all,' Patrick said, shaking his head. 'I'm sure between him and his paymasters that they have their own network of spies and informants all over Europe.'

Eva rocked back in her seat, her mind racing. 'Could it really have been that easy for him?'

'Must have been. Both Jeffrey and Adrian are dead, aren't they?'

'What about the others? The other retired agents in the UK who know about what Elliott is planning?' said Decker. He placed his hands on the table and glared at each of them. 'Well? We have to warn them, don't we?'

Patrick took a final drag on his cigarette, blew the smoke at the ceiling and then ground out the butt in an already overflowing ashtray in the middle of the table.

'That's the problem. I'm the only one left.' He gestured to the small apartment. 'Not that hiding is a problem. They're hardly going to launch a missile attack on me all the time I'm in the middle of the city, are they?'

Decker shot Eva a glance, then cleared his throat and turned back to Leavey.

'That's why we're taking you to North Africa.'

CHAPTER FORTY

London

'Chief – got a minute?'

Miles poked his head around the corner of Knox's office, his words breathless after sprinting along the corridor from the operations centre.

The Section chief glanced up from his computer screen, then beckoned to him.

'Thanks.' Miles crossed the room and collapsed into one of the armchairs opposite him.

'Nathan's just reported in – they found Leavey holed up in an apartment in Lisbon.'

Knox exhaled and pushed his keyboard away. 'It's about time we had a breakthrough.'

'There's more.' Miles took a deep breath. 'Leavey

says Elliott Wilder is behind all this – and that he's a Russian spy.'

There was a pause, a beat, a split second where Knox's mouth dropped open.

'Jesus Christ,' he managed. 'For how long?'

'Leavey reckons since he was at university in the seventies.'

Knox's jaw clenched. 'We need to act fast, Miles. This can't go public.'

'I realise that, Chief. Hang on.' Miles walked back to the door, closed it, then pulled down the blind on the window beside it, ignoring the curious glances from passing Section staff.

'You have a plan?' said Knox as he returned to his seat.

'We think we do.' Miles took a moment to compose his thoughts. Knox was likely to agree, but he needed to set out the steps to be taken with clarity – after all, it would be Knox's job on the line if it went wrong.

He bit back a snort.

If it went wrong, they'd all be looking for new jobs.

And a new country to live in if they wanted to avoid spending the rest of their lives in a remote prison with no prospect of release.

'Time is evidently of the essence,' said Knox, folding his hands under his chin and leaning his elbows on the desk, 'so spit it out.'

'Here's the thing. We knew whoever was behind all

this was anticipating a replacement shipment of four Hellfire missiles. We know they've used three from the original shipment, and potentially have one left. They have a drone – my team have narrowed it down to one that was downed in Syria two years ago and was likely sold on the black market through Russian arms dealers—'

'—Whereupon Elliott Wilder got his hands on it,' interrupted Knox, 'and probably for a special price if what you're telling me about him is true.'

'It's true,' said Miles, his voice firm. 'We've gone through some back channels to obtain access to MI6's files at the time. Leavey's right – they had a watching brief on him for nearly fifteen years before placing him on a reduced threat list.'

Knox frowned. 'How did they miss the fact he'd been activated? Surely someone was reviewing that file from time to time.'

'Understaffed, and not enough funding,' said Miles with a shrug. 'Same old story. We're trying to liaise with security services in the countries along the route we've got agreements in place with to try to intercept it.'

'How close are you?'

Miles grimaced.

'It's going to be tight. After all, Wilder's had a week's head start on us – as soon as he heard the original shipment had been intercepted, he likely organised replacements to save face. And our negotiations with those other countries' security services are ongoing. They need reassuring that they're not going to be Elliott's next target if we can't stop him.'

'Where is Elliott at the moment?'

'In hiding after leaving London. We believe he might be at one of his homes along the Mediterranean coastline so we've got teams on that. As soon as we locate him, you'll be the first to know.'

'And Delacourt?'

'She and her team – including Leavey – are on their way to Algeria. They're leaving Lisbon now, and should be in place within thirty-six hours. As soon as they're at the GPS coordinates we've agreed, we'll encrypt a message through the dark web about where Patrick Leavey can be found.' Miles sat back, adrenalin already kicking into his veins, as it did before every mission. 'Elliott won't be able to resist. As soon as that rogue drone of his is within the range of our counter-measures, we'll strike.'

'What's the fallout likely to be?'

'We've got people in Algiers ready to start spreading disinformation via the news wires within ten minutes of mission completion. The ambassador will be prepped in time for his meeting with the Algerian foreign ministry, and our intelligence suggests that it'll be old news within twelve hours.'

'All right. Good.' Knox pushed back his chair, gathered his papers together, and reached for his desk phone. 'I'll get onto the Prime Minister's office and request an urgent meeting with her tonight.'

Miles rose to his feet and straightened his tie. 'Do you think she'll agree to it?'

'She has to, doesn't she?' Knox pursed his lips. 'If Elliott isn't stopped from handing over that drone, we're going to be at war within a matter of months. She won't be able to stand by if the Middle East disintegrates, along with all the NATO accords and agreements our government has negotiated since World War Two. It'll be an unmitigated disaster.'

Miles sighed. 'I'm glad you're having that conversation with her, and not me.'

Knox opened his briefcase, shoved the paperwork inside, and then tucked his mobile phone into his jacket pocket. 'In the meantime, get yourself back to the ops room and let them know to be in position and await further instructions within twenty-four hours. We have assets in Tunisia and Libya who can help them, haven't we?'

'One or two that I might be able to rustle up if we need to.'

'Contact them as well. Just in case.' Knox frowned. 'We're only going to have one shot at this, Miles. We can't afford to screw it up.'

'Understood.'

Miles turned away as the Section chief murmured instructions into his phone and requested that Harris be ready with a car outside within two minutes, his thoughts already turning to the strategic decisions that would have to be made in order to mobilise their North African team.

Given the plan, he would have to keep them at a safe distance while ensuring someone was ready to whisk Eva and her team out of the country if it all went wrong.

Or if they succeeded and needed to be repatriated before the locals found them.

Either way, it would be risky.

'Miles?'

'Chief?' Miles paused at the door, his hand on the frame.

Knox had his hand over the receiver, his brow furrowed. 'This Patrick Leavey fellow – is he all right with this?'

'Seems to be.'

CHAPTER FORTY-ONE

Spain

Eva peered between the front seats of the dilapidated Land Rover at the reflection in the rear-view mirror of the bruising to Decker's face.

At least his lip had stopped bleeding before they had left Leavey's house.

The punch had come from nowhere, the old MI6 agent taking Decker unawares before clutching his own hand in ill-disguised pain.

'Bait? Is that what I am now? How fucking dare you—' he'd raged.

After calming him, Eva had explained the rest of the plan while Nathan patched up Decker's split lip and tried to persuade the assassin not to kill the man who posed the one decent chance they had to stop the rogue drone.

Leavey had dressed his own knuckles, cursing under his breath while they finalised details with Miles in hushed tones.

Now, the small group travelled in silence as the four-by-four travelled along a rock-strewn narrow road twisting its way south towards Tarifa, the sun setting to their right across an undulating landscape.

The headlights cut through a dusty twilight, moths smashing into the windscreen as Decker changed gear and powered the vehicle up another incline.

Leavey sat behind Decker, his jaw clenched while he stoically ignored the three of them.

'Another couple of miles and we should start dropping back down to the coast,' Nathan murmured. He rummaged in his backpack in the footwell of the passenger seat, then held four British passports over his shoulder. 'Spares, all with your photos in. Patrick – your photo is a composite from ones I could find on file, but it should pass muster.'

Leavey took it from him without a word, thumbed through the pages, then grunted under his breath. 'This is good. Better than anything they used to give me.'

Eva noticed Nathan straighten in his seat.

What the intelligence officer lacked in brawn, he more than made up for in his ability to support them in other ways, and she wouldn't trust anyone else.

With Nathan's skills at creating new identities, their passage to Morocco and then onwards to Algeria would hopefully go unnoticed by all except the Section team in London.

She hoped.

'Why was Jeffrey working undercover in the Foreign Office?' she said.

'He had this notion that someone there might be involved to start with,' said Patrick, twisting in his seat. 'It didn't take us long to create a backstory for him, and Adrian knew someone who could rustle together the paperwork he needed. Once he was in, he realised it wasn't a government traitor but one of the contractors that was involved.'

'How many people knew about him?' said Nathan. 'I mean, knew that he was under cover?'

'Obviously one person too many,' said Decker. 'Otherwise, he'd still be alive.'

'We were working alone,' said Patrick, rubbing his chest while he turned his gaze to the window. 'The likes of me, Jeffrey and Adrian are considered dinosaurs these days. We couldn't even get a meeting with the head of MI6 organised if we wanted to. That's why we decided to pool our resources and gather as much evidence as we could before we tried to raise the alarm.'

'How did you find out about the drone?'

'Adrian heard a rumour while working for his NGO in Aleppo about a Reaper that was retrieved from the hills after a coalition attack on Syrian forces. The place was remote, and we can only assume whoever was in charge of that mission assumed – wrongly – that it had been destroyed.'

'And Elliott Wilder?'

'It took us a while to trace the eventual drone purchase and the missile thefts to him – that's when we discovered he was trading on the black market as well as managing his legitimate arms business. We were trying to find out how Elliott has been ransacking the shipments,' said Patrick. He looked sickened for a moment, and sighed. 'We had no idea we'd become targets ourselves.'

'Face it – you had no idea where Dukes was, or that he was dead.' Decker looked in the rear view mirror at Eva and raised an eyebrow. 'What a fucking disaster.'

'It is, you're right. Although…' Patrick frowned.

'What is it?' said Eva.

'Jeffrey was seeing someone – one of the women who work in the office at the Department for International Trade. I wondered… I mean, I've heard nothing from Jeffrey even though he assured me he would keep me up to date about his movements once he left Ankara. Adrian never reported hearing from him again either, which is why we suspected the worst.'

'Do you think Jeffrey might have contacted her?' said Nathan.

'It's a long shot, I know…'

'What's her name?'

'Charlotte Hughes.'

'We'll let the Section know,' said Eva. 'Let's face it – we need all the help we can get at the moment, and if Jeffrey managed to get information to her without Elliott Wilder finding out, it's the best chance we've got of stopping him.'

'I'll put a call through to Knox,' said Nathan, and sighed. 'At least if we get blown to smithereens in the middle of the desert, they've still got a way to get to him if Patrick's right.'

'Do it.' Checking her watch, Eva raised her voice over the engine. 'Decker, the next ferry for Morocco leaves in an hour. Reckon we can make it?'

The vehicle surged forward as he stomped on the accelerator.

'I don't see why not.'

CHAPTER FORTY-TWO

Miles paced the thin carpet at the top of the staircase and watched while Emily crouched in front of the door to Charlotte Hughes' apartment, her jaw set in concentration.

Behind her a matching door remained closed, ignored by the Section analyst as she drilled the second of two deadlocks the parliamentary administrative assistant had fixed to hers and swore under her breath.

He fought down the adrenalin and tried to ignore his rising heart rate, then peered at his wristwatch.

Charlotte's neighbour had left the building two minutes ago.

A team of four was now tracking the man's movements towards Finsbury Park station, ready to raise the alarm if he turned back before Miles and Emily had concluded their business.

'Why couldn't he have a normal job like everyone else?' he muttered under his breath.

Discovering that the neighbour ran an IT consultancy from home, the entire group of analysts had groaned with frustration – until Jason created a diversion by way of a new client who required an urgent meeting that afternoon in a Southwark café.

They had an hour at most before the neighbour discovered his prospective client didn't exist and turned back home.

'We're in,' Emily hissed.

'Thank Christ for that.'

He hurried across the landing as she placed her hand on the door and shoved it open and then peered down at his colleague.

'I'll go first. Just in case.'

She nodded, said nothing, and fell into step behind him as he eased through the door and into a modest sized living room.

The design of the apartment was open plan with the kitchen off to his left. Artwork covered the plain-coloured walls and he recalled from the briefing notes that Emily had put together prior to their visit that Charlotte was currently renting the property, and had been doing so prior to applying for her role with the Department for International Trade.

According to the financial audit that Greg processed that morning, Charlotte had never purchased a house –

her previous home had been in her husband's name only, and he had kept that house following their divorce.

The sweet smell of fresh flowers drew his attention to the kitchen worktop and the crystal vase filled with white lilies, a scattering of fallen petals on the granite surface beside a half-empty bottle of red wine.

An oak coffee table in front of two three-seater sofas was clear except for a tidy pile of magazines off to one side that had a distinct interior design flavour to them.

'Okay,' he said. 'I'll take the bedroom and bathroom, as quick as you can, we're looking for anything that belongs to Jeffrey Dukes. And anything that might help us find out what earth he was up to. No longer than twenty minutes, so don't hang around.'

'Got it.'

While Emily wandered across to the bookshelf and began sifting between the pages of paperback titles, Miles turned on his heel and hurried along a short hallway into Charlotte's bedroom.

A double bed took up most of the space, with fitted wardrobes along the far wall and a double-glazed window overlooking the neighbouring properties.

He froze for a moment, then realised that with the weak sunlight shining on the net curtains covering the panes he wouldn't be seen. Galvanised into action, cognisant of the time passing, he pulled protective gloves from the inside pocket of his leather jacket and opened the wardrobe doors.

Charlotte was organised, that much was clear.

Work clothes were colour-coordinated and hanging from a rail to the left of the wardrobe, whereas the right-hand side was kept for casual wear. Her shoes – a variety of heels, running shoes and ankle boots – were lined up along the floor beneath the clothes.

Miles leaned closer and sank his fingers into each of the pockets of the shirts, jackets and jeans before reaching up and doing the same with the collection of handbags on the top shelf.

Nothing.

He closed the doors and turned to face the bed. There was a nightstand each side, but only one appeared to be in use, with a half-empty glass of water and a hardback first edition lying beside a small reading lamp.

He crossed to the unused nightstand, its bare surface clean, and pulled out the single drawer underneath.

Empty, save for an abandoned ballpoint pen.

Moving around the bed, he opened the drawer beneath and carefully lifted the contents, sifting through old birthday cards from colleagues whose names he recognised from Greg's research and scribbled notes about holiday ideas and the like.

Frustrated, he pushed the drawer closed and straightened.

There was nothing in the bedroom belonging to Jeffrey Dukes, and nothing to suggest that he had even been there.

He cast his gaze around the room to make sure his presence would go unnoticed, then checked his watch.

Ten minutes had already passed, and he wanted them out of here as soon as possible.

'We'll give it another five minutes, Em,' he called.

'Okay.'

He pushed open the door into a compact bathroom and paused on the threshold to get his bearings.

There was no room for a bath – the apartment's layout only allowed for a washbasin, toilet and shower cubicle. A single mirror-fronted cabinet hung on the wall above the basin, but after sifting through boxes containing tampons, painkillers and plasters, Miles realised the search had been a waste of time.

He shut the cabinet, and then jumped back with a start at the sound of a splintering crash from the kitchen.

Racing along the hallway, he found Emily standing beside the central worktop, her eyes stricken.

The remnants of the crystal vase lay in smithereens at her feet, water pooling towards the cabinets and the flowers strewn across the tiles.

'I'm sorry, Miles,' she managed. 'I turned… my elbow must've caught it…'

'Quiet,' he said, raising his hand. 'Don't panic.'

'Sorry.'

'Are you hurt?'

'No.'

'That's something, then.'

'Shit,' said Emily, her eyes wide. 'What do we do now?'

Miles cast his gaze around the room, resigned that there was no evidence to suggest Jeffrey Dukes had contacted Charlotte Hughes prior to his murder, and then turned back to his analyst.

'Did you find anything at all to link this place to Jeffrey Dukes or what he was up to?'

'No.'

'Right. Time to improvise, then.'

CHAPTER FORTY-THREE

Eva rested her elbows on the stainless steel railing encircling the upper deck of the crowded ferry and watched as the lights from Tarifa twinkled on the fringes of the pitch black coastline.

A breeze tugged at her hair, a salty taste to the air clinging to her lips. Diesel fumes wafted from the ship's exhausts, so she tilted her head away and took a deep breath.

She wouldn't move from here, though.

Not yet.

Raising her gaze to the night sky, she took in the splash of stars and checked the ferry's direction of travel before glancing over her shoulder at the sound of approaching footsteps.

'Thought I might find you out here,' said Nathan.

'How are Decker and Leavey getting on?'

'They haven't killed each other yet, although Decker refuses to let him smoke and confiscated his cigarette lighter. Meanwhile, Leavey's complaining about the food – reckons he's got the worst case of indigestion he's ever had.'

'Jesus. They're as bad as each other.'

'Think he'll do it?'

'Leavey, you mean?' She smiled. 'Yes. He's like us, isn't he? It's second nature to want to help, despite everything.'

Turning her back to the view, Eva looked down the gangway to a group of men who were gathered beside a lifeboat, a fog of smoke above their heads as they laughed and joked.

They wore the clothes of men who drifted, men who worked where they could find work, and whose lined faces bore the strain of going without too often.

'I think he'll do it, once he's had a chance to get over the shock,' she said eventually.

'I thought Decker was going to kill him.'

She grinned. 'So did I.'

'Are you going to try to get some rest? We've got a long way to go yet.'

Wrinkling her nose, she caught a whiff of marijuana from the assembled group and drew Nathan away, leading him further along the deck towards the prow of the ferry.

'We should take turns catching some sleep,' she

said. 'If Leavey's got his head down and Decker's keeping watch at the moment, then we'll swap with them in a couple of hours. How are you holding up?'

He shot her a rueful smile. 'Oh, you know. Getting used to being shot at again.'

'I'm sorry.'

'It was too good to be true, wasn't it?' He peered out into the darkness. 'I mean, I really had convinced myself for a while there that I was just a bookstore owner.'

Eva reached out and squeezed his hand. 'You're a good bookstore owner.'

'At least I didn't let you burn it down.'

'There's that.' She sighed. 'Although I don't know what we're going to do with the place after all this.'

'Are you worried that word will get around and we'll get bombarded with requests for help?'

'I don't mind that so much. It's knowing that the Section know where I am.'

Nathan shrugged. 'Maybe, once all this is over, Knox will leave us alone.'

'I doubt that.'

'Why?'

'We're not exactly at the top of his Christmas card list at the moment, are we?'

CHAPTER FORTY-FOUR

Charlotte bit back the yelp of pain as the man's elbow caught her in the ribs before he extracted himself from the seat beside her, his sour body odour wafting through the bus as he joined the queue to leave.

She rubbed her side and checked the zip on her handbag was still closed, glaring at him as he climbed off and passed the window, his head down.

The bus pulled away, and she risked a glance over her shoulder.

The woman behind her was holding up her mobile phone, the screen almost touching her nose as she poked and prodded at it, her brow furrowed.

An elderly man next to the woman held a book in one hand, the other dipping into a bag of crisps, his attention completely taken by the sports biography he was reading.

He glanced up and Charlotte turned away slowly, pretending to crane her neck over the heads of the other passengers and checking her watch.

Once she was sure she wasn't being observed by the other passengers, she unzipped her bag and pulled out the envelope that Jeffrey had sent.

Extracting his notes, she flipped the map and news articles between her fingers, sorting through the handwritten pages until she found the photograph.

Three men.

Three descriptions.

She'd heard the rumours now, and had put the pieces together from the fractured conversations she had been listening to all day at Whitehall Place.

Jeffrey Dukes – not dead from a heart attack, but in a suspected missile attack.

Adrian Ogilvy – also dead, with all reports pointing to another missile attack.

One more man.

Charlotte ran her fingernail under the description for him, then reached into her bag once more and extracted her notebook. Snapping away the elastic to free the cover, she shook the pages until a photograph tumbled out.

It had been printed from an old newspaper report about a spy ring that had been broken in Brussels in the early eighties.

It had taken some planning, and login details

belonging to a junior administrator, but a search through the archives after hours had finally proven fruitful.

She ignored the politicians in the foreground of the photo, their faces conveying the shock at discovering how close they had come to being infiltrated.

Instead, she peered at the man in the background, the one who was holding the door open to a sleek limousine, his body language that of someone on edge, ready to strike.

He wasn't named in the accompanying caption, but as Charlotte read Jeffrey's description and looked at the photograph once more, she finally recognised him.

'Patrick Leavey,' she whispered. 'Well, well, well.'

It had been twenty years since she'd crossed paths with the man – and that had been fleetingly. She had been a secretary, after all, and of little consequence to the men in power.

But she remembered him.

Her head snapped up as the bus driver braked, smudged away the condensation on the window with her coat sleeve, and cursed under her breath as she recognised her stop.

Shoving the papers back into the envelope and zipping shut her bag, she pushed her way to the front of the bus, apologising as she knocked against other passengers in her haste to reach the door before it swished closed.

The driver glared at her in his mirror, his hand hovering over the button when she drew near.

'Sorry.'

She shot him an apologetic smile and launched herself onto the pavement, the doors closing seconds before the bus roared away.

The walk to the flat only took a couple of minutes, her breath fogging in the night air while her heels clacked along the uneven pavers.

Jeffrey's notes, the men's names, the unanswered questions that remained – all jostled for her attention as she keyed in the passcode for the ground floor security door and stepped inside.

There was a weariness in her step by the time she climbed the last stair tread and shoved her hand in her bag, wrapping her fingers around her house keys.

The smell of frying garlic and onion wafted from under her neighbour's door, a tinkle of laughter and murmured voices interrupting the tumbling thoughts that occupied her every waking moment.

The Minister's office had been a hub of frantic activity all day, and although she suspected it had something to do with the man who had arrived unannounced the previous day demanding to speak with Edward Toskins, she didn't have the security clearances or the nerve to ask Neil Hodges what was going on.

Instead, she had lurked in corridors, hovered at doorways and tried to listen to the fleeting snatches of conversation passing her by as, one by one, the Minister's advisers and acolytes were called into his office.

They didn't stay long.

Five minutes, ten if they were having a particularly bad day, and they came hurrying away. They avoided eye contact, kept their heads down and scurried out into the corridors of Whitehall Place as if someone had lit a firecracker under their backsides.

At least she had been included in the subsequent meetings with the department's patrons and contractors. Out of all of them, Elliott Wilder had impressed her the most – not least because of the nonchalant way he had dismissed Hodges and Toskins for what they were.

A lot of hot air.

Charlotte sighed as she raised her key to the door of her apartment, then froze.

She ran her hand over the grazes to the paintwork, scratch marks that tore at the seam between the door and the frame.

Jaw set, she pushed against the door.

It didn't move.

'What the hell…'

Frowning, she inserted the key and held her breath.

The lock turned easily, undamaged.

Any hope that whoever tried to break into her apartment had failed faded the instant she pushed open the door.

Charlotte staggered against the doorframe, her mouth open as her eyes took in the sheer devastation.

The living room had been torn to pieces – cushions lay strewn over the carpet, the bookshelves had been emptied of their contents and books tossed to the floor, and as she picked her way through to the kitchen, she held a shaking hand to her lips.

The crystal vase her mother had given her lay in smithereens across the tiled floor, the last stems from a bouquet of lilies Jeffrey had presented her with the night before he left now withering in a pool of water.

Cupboards had been wrenched open, as if whoever did this was in a hurry, with crockery and glassware splintered over the tiles, crunching under her shoes.

She backed away, then hurried to her bedroom and let out a shocked gasp.

The intruder had been here, too.

Heart hammering, Charlotte turned back to the living room and placed her handbag on the coffee table.

She had never been burgled before, so why now?

She set her shoulders, and unzipped the bag, peering in at the envelope.

Was that what the intruders were looking for?

Who were they?

She spun around at noise out in the corridor beyond her front door, then gulped a deep breath when she realised it was only another neighbour returning from work.

She had taken too long already – she needed to phone the police, report the break-in and ascertain if anything had been taken, despite the knowledge that the intruder was likely after the documents she had been carrying in her bag for safe-keeping.

As she picked up her mobile phone, she hurried along the short hallway and into the bedroom once more.

She stopped at the foot of the bed, the sheets strewn across the mattress and the three drawers beside her wardrobe ripped open, her personal effects tossed over the floor.

She glanced down, her thumb hovering over the emergency button at the base of the phone screen.

Biting her lip, she threw the mobile onto the dressing table and then began to pick up the underwear and jewellery that had been discarded over the carpet beside the open doors of her wardrobe.

'Whoever you are, you bastards,' she hissed under her breath. 'You'll pay for this.'

CHAPTER FORTY-FIVE

Gerald Knox paused beside a gilt-framed mirror, adjusted his tie with a grimace, then dropped his hand as a door to his left opened and one of the Prime Minister's staff beckoned to him.

'Good luck,' he murmured as Knox passed.

Knox pursed his lips.

It wasn't the first time he had woken the PM after midnight, but it had been a while – and she wasn't known for being gracious at that time of day.

He blinked to let his eyes adjust to the soft lighting from the table lamps in the study as the door closed behind him, then noticed a figure already sitting in one of the armchairs at the far end.

'This had better be good, Knox.'

'Good evening, Prime Minister.'

'It certainly was, until twenty minutes ago.' She

waved him to the chair beside her, and indicated two crystal tumblers on the table between them. 'I presume you'll join me in a nightcap.'

'Thank you, Prime Minister.'

They clinked glasses, and Knox savoured the smooth single malt for a moment before resting the glass on his knee.

Eventually, she spoke. 'All right, what's going on?'

'We've made significant progress with the matters we discussed, and my team have located a former MI6 agent by the name of Patrick Leavey who is assisting us. Leavey has indicated to my team that the person behind this is known to the British government.'

'Who?'

Knox lowered his voice. 'Elliott Wilder.'

'Shit.' The Prime Minister closed her eyes for a moment, then sighed. 'Do you think Nivens or Toskins – or anyone in their departments is involved?'

'No, Prime Minister. Robert Nivens gave us no cause for concern – he has very little to do with the day-to-day running of the Foreign Office and tends to delegate, and I don't think Toskins has a clue as to what's been going on.' He emitted a snort. 'We think that's why Dukes first joined the FCO – he might've thought the arms thefts were an inside job, but that's until he uncovered Elliott's involvement.'

'Any idea how many shipments were compromised?'

'We have eight confirmed so far, all over a period of fourteen months. Last week's missile theft was the first on that scale though. From what we can deduce, it's been a mixture of surface-to-air rocket launchers, small arms and landmines until now.'

'So, whatever he's up to, he's been planning it for a while. That would explain why he viewed both Dukes and Ogilvy as threats.'

'We've conducted an in-depth analysis of everyone working in the Department for International Trade and apart from a few questionable deals to countries that have slipped through the net with regard to arms sales, we're confident that they're in the clear as far as Elliott Wilder is concerned.'

She opened her eyes, and gave a slight shake of her head as if clearing any negative thoughts. Her voice held a brusqueness to it when she spoke. 'Next steps?'

'I spoke to my team an hour ago. They're currently based in North Africa – Algiers, to be exact.'

'Why there?'

'With respect, Prime Minister, I will get to that. However, you should also be aware that we have every reason to believe that Elliott Wilder is an active Russian agent.'

Even in the warm glow from the lamps placed around the room, he could see her face pale.

'Our situation worsens.' Her hand shook as she lowered her glass to her lap. 'Are you sure?'

'Yes. Patrick Leavey – the contact that Delacourt's team located in Portugal – confirms that Wilder first came under suspicion in the eighties but MI6 never managed to pull together enough evidence to bring him in. Notwithstanding that, Wilder has managed to inveigle himself into being awarded numerous arms contracts since the early nineties, whittling away at those suspicions by stealth.'

'He's determined.'

'He's patient.' Knox couldn't help the note of admiration in his voice. 'As is the case with many Russian agents, he and his masters are in this for the long haul, hence why he's been careful. Obviously, something has triggered this sudden course of action though. It seems extreme by comparison to his previous strategy of lying low.'

The Prime Minister waved her hand in front of her face as if batting away an errant fly. 'Europe is dealing with some of the biggest challenges it's faced in fifty years. It's the perfect time for the Russians to take advantage of the instability we're facing. Perhaps Elliott and those controlling him decided it was time to make a power grab.'

'We have a plan to deal with this matter, but it is a little… unorthodox,' said Knox, tapping his fingers against his glass as he waited for her reaction.

Eventually, she narrowed her eyes at him. 'I'm not going to like this, am I?'

'It'll afford us a quick and easy solution, Prime Minister. One that won't involve your detractors. One that can be – up to a point, at least – kept out of the public eye until it becomes absolutely necessary to make a statement. And one that can be set in motion immediately.'

'Tell me.'

Knox set out the plan as the PM listened without interruption.

'Prime Minister, I realise this is extreme, but I believe it's the only way to resolve the situation. If we try to apprehend Elliott Wilder there is a very real risk that he'll escape. If he does, and he manages to head back to Russia, the political fallout could be disastrous for you.' Knox paused. 'Killing Wilder is the only viable option.'

When he was finished, she took a sip of her drink and gazed at the carpet for a moment before speaking.

'There's no other way?'

'Not without the involvement of MI6 or the MoD, no.'

Her lips twisted. 'As you know, I'd rather they didn't know. Not yet.'

'Understood, Prime Minister.' Knox turned in his chair to face her. 'My team of analysts here in London have run the projections on this, along with several other scenarios. It's our best chance.'

'Very well.'

'I take it then, Prime Minister, that I can have your authority to proceed on the basis I've just outlined?'

She drained her drink, then placed the glass on the table and rose to her feet.

Knox stood, towering over the diminutive woman who held the country's future in her hands, and held his breath.

Her gaze moved to the bookcases lining the walls, to the tomes of case law, history and geography, before finding him once more.

'Do it.'

'Thank you, Prime Minister.'

He shook her hand, then made a hasty retreat across the study, his mind already turning to the intricacies of the operation.

'Knox?'

He paused, and glanced over his shoulder. 'Prime Minister?'

'For goodness' sakes, tell them to keep the damage to a minimum this time.'

CHAPTER FORTY-SIX

Morocco

Eva shielded her eyes against the glare off the windscreen, then held up her mobile phone and swore under her breath.

Pulling down a baseball cap to afford some shade over her pale features, she flicked up the collar of her polo shirt and wandered back to the four-by-four.

'I've still got no signal.'

'Doesn't matter. I don't think the breakdown service will come out here anyway,' muttered Decker from under the vehicle.

His legs poked out from under the radiator grille, his body lying in a narrow trench that they'd dug into the stony track – back-breaking work that had taken the four of them almost an hour using their hands and shoes to scrape away the dirt and pebbles.

Nathan crouched beside him, a toolbox at his feet while Leavey lay prone beside the front wheels, pointing a torch at whatever Decker was trying to fix.

'How's it going?' she said.

'Nearly got it.' A clang sounded from underneath the Land Rover. 'Fuck. Maybe not.'

Eva pursed her lips, tucking her phone back into her pocket and resisting the urge to check her watch.

They had left Tangiers as soon as the ferry had docked, the journey from Spain leaving her frustrated and on edge. She had taken turns with the others to keep watch while they each snatched a few precious hours of rest, but the lack of information from London about the shipment of replacement missiles created an underlying sense of urgency that she couldn't shake.

She exhaled and turned away, scanning the horizon for signs of approaching traffic.

Eight hours on decrepit roads like these in a vehicle that had been used for little more than a run-around during Leavey's time in Portugal was bound to have its difficulties, but they could've done without the sudden grinding noise that made Decker stomp on the brakes and haul the Land Rover over to the side of the narrow track.

They had to get Patrick over the border and into

Algeria – it was the only way they could make Knox's plan work.

If a drone strike took place on Moroccan soil, they would never hear the end of it.

She pivoted, turning her attention to the snaking path of the road as it twisted and curved across the rock-strewn hillsides bare except for scrubby grass-like shrubs clinging to the base of rocks and boulders.

Another *clang* resonated off the front axle of the Land Rover behind her.

'Got it.'

Eva wandered back as Decker wiggled out from underneath the four-by-four, his face covered with oil spatter, grease and dirt.

He grinned as Nathan handed him a bottle of water and a T-shirt, drank some before tipping the rest over his head, then wiped his face. 'It's going to get bumpy the rest of the way, but we'll get there.'

'What was it?' said Eva as Leavey reached out and helped him to his feet.

'Front radius arm and Panhard rod.' Decker dusted himself off as Nathan picked up the rudimentary tools and began throwing them in the back of the vehicle. 'Hopefully the tyres will hold up, but it'll sound worse than it is.'

Leavey rubbed his chest, sweat patches under his arms as he squinted into the distance. 'If we're going to get to that rendezvous before afternoon, we should get going. I've topped up the fuel tank, so we won't need to stop again for a few hundred miles.' He reached into the vehicle and extracted another water bottle before taking a mouthful, running the back of his hand across his mouth afterwards. 'I can take the first driving shift, if you like.'

'I'll drive,' said Eva. 'You all need to rest, given the past few hours. You look worn out.'

He flashed her a smile. 'I'm fine.'

'Then let's go,' said Eva, and climbed into the driver's seat. She swore as the hot leather burned through her jeans, turned the key in the ignition and waited until the other three had settled in for the ride.

If they could circumvent the border at Oujda and get to Saïda tonight, then they would be able to set out early to make the final journey to the location Nathan had identified with his sister's help out in the Algerian desert.

Somewhere isolated.

Somewhere far away from prying eyes.

Somewhere no-one would hear the noise from a MQ-9 Reaper as its weapons found their target.

CHAPTER FORTY-SEVEN

London

Miles rolled up his shirtsleeves as he paced the windowless operations room, cricked his neck and stared up at the large screens taking up the length of the wall.

Greg and Emily had split the display so that one half gave them a satellite view of Eva's progress, and the other a live camera feed from a Section team on the ground in Malta.

Miles kept his attention on the view from the team leader's vest-mounted camera.

Olly Maxwell had been recruited from the British Army three days before accepting an offered role with the SAS six years ago, and was the only man Knox would entrust the mission.

Capable, dependable, with the ability to strategise with split-second decisiveness, he was a natural choice.

Behind Maxwell, visible from a satellite feed hovering over the harbour, were three men in identical tactical clothing. One British and two Maltese hurriedly recruited from the island's police firearms unit once the necessary agreements had been made with the government there.

Maxwell had handpicked them as soon as he'd read their service records.

Beyond the harbour, two vessels owned by the Maltese authorities were maintaining watch on the ensuing operation from the water.

If Maxwell's team failed to take control of the Hellfire missiles, all shipping would be prevented from leaving Marsaxlokk in an attempt to stop Elliott's smuggling operation from entering international waters.

'Do you think the captain of that ship knows the cargo's a target?' said Emily, passing him a copy of the latest report.

Miles took one last look at the screen, then flipped open the manila folder. 'It depends whether he's part of the smuggling operation. If someone diverted his attention away from the ship while the container was breached last time, then no – but we'll be sure to ask him.'

The young analyst smiled. 'I wouldn't mind listening to that conversation.'

'Careful what you wish for,' he said, then frowned as he sifted through the contents of the folder. 'Is this what I think it is?'

Emily tapped her finger on the satellite photo in his hand. 'That's Elliott's drone. We traced it from Bulgaria over the border into Turkey about half an hour ago.'

'So the missiles are definitely heading there.'

'That's my thinking, which is why this ship has to be the one the missiles have been smuggled onto. When it leaves Malta, it ends up in İzmir in three days' time before turning for home.'

'And from İzmir, Elliott and his client will be able to transport them by road to the waiting drone.' Miles slapped the folder shut and handed it back to her. 'This is good work.'

'As long as we stop the missiles from being stolen this time.'

He saw her brow furrow as she turned back to the screens, and exhaled. 'It's good intelligence work, Emily.'

'Hope so.' She flashed him a small smile before returning to her computer.

'Me too,' he muttered, then: 'Greg – open a line through to Maxwell for me.'

Within seconds, the team leader's voice came

through speakers set into the ceiling of the operations room.

'Newcombe?'

'Time to go, Maxwell. Everything all right there?'

'We've got movement on the front deck. There are a couple of locals on the quay, but the ship's been moored at the far end so it's quieter. She's not due to be unloaded for another half an hour.'

'Tell your men to keep their distance,' said Miles. 'We can't afford to alert Wilder or his people to their presence until we know he's used the last remaining Hellfire. We have to make sure he targets Leavey, otherwise God knows what else he might do with it.'

'Understood,' said Maxwell. 'Standing by.'

Miles turned to Emily. 'Where's our drone?'

'The pilots confirm they're prepared for take-off,' the analyst replied. 'Once they're in the air and out of Swiss airspace, they'll head south towards the Mediterranean, at which point we'll bring Marie online to take control of the weapons guidance system from here.'

Miles signalled to Greg to cut the connection.

From now on, they would only hear the sparse chatter between the four men on the ground once they moved from their position ready to begin the targeted assault and search.

Maxwell was now in command of that part of the

operation, with no further input from the Section's London headquarters.

'Are the Maltese officials ready as well?' said Miles. 'They need to get their story straight – Elliott must be led to believe that the missiles are in the hands of his people. He'll be waiting for their signal.'

'Yes, they're listening in as well,' said Emily.

'Okay.' Miles crossed his arms over his chest and battened down the adrenalin, his heart racing.

Everything hinged on the next step – persuading Elliott Wilder to use his last remaining missile so that the drone would be useless without its reinforcements.

Greg looked up from his computer screen, his finger hovering over the mouse button. 'Ready when you are.'

Miles turned his attention to the satellite images displayed on the wall, his gaze roaming the desert beyond the Algerian coastline, and then exhaled.

'Send the message.'

CHAPTER FORTY-EIGHT

Algeria

'He's dead.'

Eva snuffled, then sat up in her seat, rubbing sleep from her eyes. 'What? Who?'

Decker was outside the vehicle, his arms resting on the open driver's window as he peered in. 'Leavey. He's dead.'

She was awake then, heart pounding as her brain tried to catch up with what she was hearing. 'When? How?'

Stumbling from the passenger seat, she half-fell out the door and then stared at the back seats.

Empty.

'Decker? What did you do?'

She stormed round to the other side, her fists clenched while she tried to work out how the hell she was going to inform London that they had lost their element of surprise, that two men had argued and that now, one of them was dead.

Decker held up his hands as she advanced on him, and took a step back. 'I didn't do anything, I swear. He said he needed to get some air, so I pulled over. He wandered off – I thought he was stopping to take a piss. Then he keeled over.'

Eva blinked, confusion turning to panic. 'Where is he?'

'Over there.' He jerked his chin towards a crumpled form by the side of the jagged rock face.

'Bloody hell.'

The assassin had parked the Land Rover beside a rocky outcrop, its crags and ridges creating a natural overhang providing some shelter from the morning sun.

She marched over to where Leavey lay a few metres away from the four-by-four, his face turned to one side and his hands outstretched as if he'd tried to break his fall.

A small scratch marked his cheek, but his features were peaceful, his eyes closed as if he were asleep.

Turning to face the road that stretched in both directions, then sweeping her gaze over the rocky terrain, she could see no evidence of anyone else passing in the hours she'd been asleep.

Besides, the others would have woken her if they were about to have company.

The whole landscape was deserted, save for them.

In the shade of the overhang, Eva swatted flies away from her face, the temperature already reaching thirty Celsius, despite it only being eight o'clock in the morning.

'Heart attack?' she said to Decker as he joined her.

'Probably the most excitement he's had in years,' said Decker.

Eva peered down at the old MI6 agent's stricken form once more. 'He never said anything about health problems, did he?'

'We didn't ask.'

She turned at the sound of Nathan's voice to see him walking over from the Land Rover, an old blanket folded over his arm.

'I found this in the back,' he said, wrinkling his nose. 'It smells a bit, but—'

'It'll have to do,' she said.

'Now what?' said Decker, and kicked at a loose stone, sending it shooting across the road and into a natural dry culvert on the other side. 'We can't bury him out here, can we? This surface is rock-solid – it was bad enough having to dig a trench yesterday to fix the—'

'Do you think that's maybe what killed him?' said Nathan. 'After all, he insisted on working as hard as us.'

Decker shrugged in response.

'Well, we can't leave him here, can we?' said Eva. 'As soon as the next vehicle drives past, he'll be discovered. A white bloke in his sixties will raise all sorts of questions – and if it hits the news, we risk Elliott Wilder finding out.'

'So shall we take him with us, then? Bury him as soon as we get a chance?'

Eva glared at him, then began shaking out the blanket and draped it over Leavey's prone body. 'We have a bigger problem at the moment. How the hell are we going to convince Wilder to use that last missile if our target is dead?'

'Maybe…' Nathan shook his head. 'No, doesn't matter.'

'Spit it out,' said Decker. 'Now.'

'Well, it's just a thought, but you don't need Leavey alive to make the plan work, do you?' he said. 'I mean, we can't phone Knox and tell him he's dead. They've already sent the message to Wilder through the dark web. All we need to do is make sure Elliott can see Patrick in the vehicle from the drone cameras, don't we? He could be asleep as far as Wilder is concerned.'

Eva searched his face for a moment before a smile twitched her lips. 'Jesus – you're a dark horse, aren't you?'

His eyes widened as he held up his hands. 'Forget I said anything.'

'Don't be ridiculous. I think it'll work.' She turned

her attention back to the horizon as a heatwave shimmered across the road in the distance, their destination within a few more hours.

'That doesn't make me feel any better.'

'What do you think, Decker?'

'It's worth a shot.'

'Do we tell Miles and Knox?'

'Hell, no,' said Decker. He bent over and picked up Leavey by the ankles. 'Come on – grab his arms. We'll prop him up on the back seat. Eva, put your baseball cap on him – like Nathan said, anyone driving past will just think he's asleep, and if Elliott does manage to trace us before we're in place, that's what he'll see as well.'

Nathan stared at the dead man beside him. 'I feel really bad about doing this to him.'

'What? He looks comfortable.'

'No, I mean using him for target practice. At least when he was alive, he knew he had a chance of escaping the drone strike.'

'Don't worry about it – he'd have done the same to you,' said Decker, and clapped his hand on his shoulder.

'Oh, thanks.'

CHAPTER FORTY-NINE

Near Vakif, Turkey

Elliott Wilder took a delicate sip of apple tea and savoured the sweet flavours while the hot glass burned his fingertips and gazed out across a barren landscape towards the sweeping waters of the Aegean Sea.

'You're sure it's him?'

He turned at the sound of his client's voice, placed the tea glass on the fold-out table beside him and smiled.

'If you'd like to view the camera angles from our drone, General Yilmaz? We should be on target within the next fifteen minutes.'

The General was burly and dressed in a Turkish army uniform, his medals clanging against his chest as he moved around the table and positioned himself beside one of the operators, thick eyebrows knitting together as he peered at the screens.

Elliott pursed his lips, then joined him.

He clenched his fists as he stood behind the General and watched as the Turkish pilot brought the Reaper out of its cruising altitude and began its final approach.

Yilmaz was unpredictable, egotistical – and ambitious.

When he had first approached him at the arms fair in Paris, Elliott had been given the impression that the General was negotiating on behalf of the Turkish government.

That soon changed once their conversations continued in private, away from prying eyes and ears.

Upon hearing the man's plans to wrest control of his country, oust the incumbent he reported to and seek to address the power balance within the Middle East, Elliott had bit back his excitement and listened.

A new war always brought new opportunities, as did any eventual peace-keeping missions, and he had seized the chance to provide the General with whatever he required.

He always knew he'd find a use for the retrofitted Reaper one day.

It had all been going smoothly until Jeffrey Dukes had been seen at the quayside in İzmir – a face that

Elliott thought had been consigned to his past, and all the secrets that went with it.

The General's insistence that all potential threats to their ordnance deal be taken care of had been frustrating but necessary, especially as the results had served to demonstrate the aircraft's power and precision.

Yilmaz had been delighted with the results so far, but everything hinged on this last mission.

To destroy the last man who knew about Elliott's past – and who could destroy his future, along with Yilmaz's coup d'état.

Elliott glanced over his shoulder to where another man sat in front of a laptop computer, his face illuminated by the screen's glow.

'Have we got satellite confirmation yet?'

'Affirmative, Mr Wilder.'

'Show me.' He moved away from the command desk as the man spun the laptop around to face him, pointing at a lone vehicle parked a few hundred metres away from a low-lying home, the rust-coloured corrugated iron roof almost blending into the soil and dust surrounding it. He grunted with satisfaction. 'Can you get any closer?'

'No, sorry, Mr Wilder. I've checked the licence plate though, and it's the same that's registered to Mr Leavey.'

'What's Leavey doing in Algeria, anyway?' Yilmaz squinted at the screen, his brow furrowed.

'We believe he thought he would intercept the missiles in Algiers,' said Elliott. 'That is what my contact in London believes based on information to hand. Of course, he is too late but we will use his mistake to our advantage. We can eliminate the last threat to your plans.'

'Very well. Proceed.'

'All right.' Elliott turned back to the drone pilot. 'Have your sensor operator confirm the identity of the driver before we strike.'

'Yes, sir.'

The General's eyes narrowed. 'Is there a problem?'

'I'm simply being careful, General Yilmaz.' Elliott spread his hands. 'We've come this far, and you have a great future ahead of you. It makes no sense to rush these things.'

The other man's shoulders relaxed, and he gave an enigmatic smile. 'You are right, of course. Are you sure I cannot persuade you to join me in this venture, Mr Wilder? Your insights would give me a great advantage, I can tell.'

'That's very kind of you to say so, General, but I'm afraid my business commitments prevent me from doing so.' Elliott grimaced. 'I would hate for there to be any, shall we say, conflict of interest.'

Yilmaz guffawed, and turned back to the drone camera screens. 'I'm sure there will be plenty of conflict to serve your interests, Mr Wilder.'

Elliott cast his gaze across the room to where a pair of heavyweight men stood, their backs to the double doors of the warehouse, a shimmer of daylight behind them.

Beyond it, a black four-by-four had been parked, the driver visible through the windscreen as he read a newspaper and waited for his passenger to return.

Three miles away, Elliott's pilot also waited for him, the private jet refuelled and ready for take-off as soon as the General released the final payment.

'And you say the British government are no wiser since your meeting with them?' called out Yilmaz.

Elliott turned to see the General peering around the side of the screen at him.

'Don't worry about the Department for International Trade,' he replied. 'My brother is still in London, negotiating on your behalf so that you'll receive additional help with financing your purchases once the coup is complete.'

'Excellent. Here – join me. Come and watch this final demonstration of our power, Mr Wilder.' The General smiled benevolently as Elliott sank into a chair beside him. 'The next time you see this happen, it will be all over your news channels as I make sure my country's place at the negotiating table is assured, together with our future.'

Elliott nodded, and wondered what the current

incumbent would think of Yilmaz's plans to rip Turkey away from Europe once and for all.

He checked his phone, wondering if he should tell the pilot to warm the engines and be ready for an immediate take-off the minute Elliott's driver delivered him to the private airfield.

Instead he exhaled, crossed his legs and watched while the drone's sensor operator began adjusting the controls and the camera feed came to life as the Reaper dropped through the low cloud cover over Algerian territory.

'How long before they track us?' murmured the General.

'We'll be in and out before they know it,' said Elliott. 'Don't worry.'

'We have got visual,' called the sensor operator.

Elliott held his breath as the camera lens zoomed in to where the Land Rover sat parked beside a rough track leading away from the ramshackle hut that they'd seen from the satellite images.

'Is it him?' The General shuffled forward, jutting his chin and squinting.

The camera zoomed in further, and Elliott blinked before taking another look.

The sensor operator had locked on to the windscreen of the four-by-four, a man's hands resting on the steering wheel.

Eyes closed, his head tilted back, he appeared to be asleep, his mouth open as if snoring.

'Do we know who he's meant to be meeting with?' said Yilmaz.

'A local,' said Elliott. 'Our intel suggests the man is a drug dealer – Leavey must be getting desperate for help after the death of his colleagues.'

'We should wait, and kill them both.'

'If we do that, we risk being caught, and the drone will be destroyed,' said Elliott, keeping his voice calm. 'It's now or never, General.'

'Do it.'

Elliott nodded at the pilot. 'You heard him.'

'Sir.' The pilot's thumb nudged the firing button, then: 'Missile released. Impact in fifty seconds, forty-nine, forty-eight…'

Yilmaz turned to Elliott, his eyes blazing. 'As soon as this is done, I want that drone back here.'

'Not a problem, General.'

'And my missiles?'

Elliott held up his phone, a new text message displayed on the screen. 'At the quayside in Malta, ready for your orders. I'm told by my contact there that they can have them on a ship to your named destination within two hours.'

The General rose from his seat, tugged at his jacket, then smiled and stuck out his giant paw of a hand.

'Then I believe we have a deal, Mr Wilder.'

CHAPTER FIFTY

Algeria

Eva wiped her forehead with her sleeve, and shifted her weight from foot to foot.

The stench of goat shit mingled with over-ripened prickly pears clinging in vain to twisted vines leaning against the tumbledown walls of the abandoned building, but the place provided shade – and a place to hide.

Several hundred metres away, far enough that shrapnel from the blast wouldn't decapitate them, sat the abandoned Land Rover.

Behind the steering wheel sat the body of Patrick Leavey.

She could see his face through the windscreen, his

pale features turning a blue hue by the time they'd reached their destination. Initial rigor mortis had passed, and she had watched as Decker and Nathan wrested the man's body into position before sprinting to join her under cover of the dilapidated building's tin roof.

Nathan hovered at her side, his nervousness radiating from him in waves sending goosebumps scuttling across her forearms.

'Any moment now,' he murmured.

She glanced over her shoulder at the sound of an engine turning over, its pitiful choked attempts filling the space.

'How're you getting on with that?' she said to Decker, who turned the ignition once more.

The engine died again.

'We did that bloke a favour buying this off him in Saïda,' he said, and shook his head. 'It's a heap of shit. No wonder he was so fucking friendly.'

Eva swallowed.

The little two-door hatchback was their only means of escape after the drone strike, the only way to try to avoid detection by any military aircraft swooping over the area in the aftermath of the explosion.

It had to work.

'They should be here by now.'

Nathan's voice roused her, and she turned back to face the Land Rover.

Were they too late?

She had faced death before, many times, but on each occasion she had at least met her opponent face to face.

She had been trained to fight – weapons, unarmed combat, poisons – but she had never been up against a threat like this.

An invisible opponent.

Behind her, the car rumbled to life.

'Thank fuck for that.' Decker slammed shut the door and wandered over to where she stood. 'If I'd known I was going to be little more than a glorified fucking mechanic…'

'Elliott's missile is incoming.' Nathan pressed an earpiece with his forefinger, and murmured a response to the Section's command centre. 'Twenty seconds to impact.'

Eva tugged him away from the open door, moving into the shadows alongside Decker, and held her breath.

They all knew what the destructive force from a Hellfire missile could do, and she had no wish to get caught up in the imminent shockwave.

'We're too close,' Nathan said through gritted teeth and peered up through the holes in the roof, dust motes spiralling in the sunlight streaming through. 'If that missile lands in the wrong place, they'll be etching our names on a memorial.'

'No they won't,' replied Decker. 'We don't exist, remember?'

Eva let their words wash over her, her mouth dry while she tried to batten down the urge to run.

Here was safer, she knew that, but the temptation to flee was almost too much.

'You'll be torn to pieces by the shrapnel, Delacourt.' Decker rested his hand on her shoulder. 'Stay where you are.'

'Ten seconds,' Nathan intoned. 'Nine… eight…'

'This was a really bad idea,' said Eva, and then followed Decker's lead and dropped to the floor in a crouch, folding her arms over her head.

Even then, the sheer noise from the blast as the weapon found its target knocked her backwards, hot air sending scorched dust and sand through the open orifices of the abandoned building.

The ground shook, a deep rumbling that seemed to emanate from the depths of the earth.

Coughing, they instinctively huddled closer together, and Eva rubbed her forearm across her eyes.

'Jesus,' she managed, her voice rasping as she sucked in a deep breath while the blast passed overhead.

Decker murmured something next to her, a look of wonder on his face as he turned and stared out the open door.

She shook her head, pointed to her ears, then followed his gaze.

The four-by-four vehicle she had seen only seconds ago had been reduced to a smoking crater several metres wide, a number of large boulders strewn across the dirt and sand that had been dislodged and spat out by the impact.

Eva coughed again, then moved to the door, making sure she kept to the shadows to avoid any prying cameras thousands of metres above her position.

'Where's ours?' she said, shielding her eyes from the sun's glare. 'Shouldn't they be close behind?'

'They'll be here,' said Nathan.

Decker's top lip curled. 'They'd bloody better be.'

CHAPTER FIFTY-ONE

London

Miles glanced over his shoulder as the door to the command centre opened and Gerald Knox walked in, his face etched with worry.

'Well?'

'Elliott's missile found its target.'

'Where's our drone?' Knox pointed at the GPS displays and satellite images projected onto the wall above their heads.

'About twenty seconds away.'

Miles used a laser pointer to show Knox where to look, then tracked the Section's drone as it pursued its quarry.

The aircraft swept across a cement factory on the

outskirts of Saïda, then banked to the right and passed over a narrow track leading away from the town.

'I need to hang back,' called Marie, 'otherwise Elliott's lot will spot us on their radar. They're still on site, maintaining an altitude of five thousand feet.'

'Do it,' said Miles to the pilot. 'Be ready to drop into position the minute you need to, though.'

'Why would they do that instead of using the camera to zoom in?' said Knox.

'Either Elliott or his client wants to make sure no-one else is around,' Miles murmured.

'Do you think they've heard about the shipment?'

'No – I don't think so. They wouldn't have risked using the last missile to take out Leavey otherwise.' Miles turned to the Section chief and grinned. 'I think our ruse worked.'

Knox's jaw clenched, then he turned back to Marie. 'Are you in position yet?'

'Yes, Chief.'

'Get the target on camera.'

Miles reached out, resting his hand on the back of his seat as the camera zoomed into its target, a sudden vertigo causing a dizziness that made him look away for a moment.

When he raised his eyes to the screen once more, he saw it.

The pale grey outline of the rogue drone, hovering above the desert landscape.

'Prepare to fire,' said Knox, his voice ringing out in the enclosed space.

'We need to strike now, Gerald,' Miles murmured. 'They could turn and be over a nearby town within minutes.'

Knox said nothing, his face passive as he watched Elliott's Reaper.

'Marie? The minute that missile's away, you need to get the hell out of there, otherwise we're going to have an Algerian MiG fighter plane on our tail,' said Miles. 'Understand, that isn't an option.'

'Copy that,' came the calm reply. 'We'll be across the border and over international waters before they can get off the ground.'

'Make sure you are.'

Knox finally held up his hand, his gaze remaining on the screens. 'Marie? You have a "go". I repeat, "go".'

He could hear the slight intake of breath from the woman at the realisation she could now wreak her revenge on the man who had killed her crew, and then she spoke.

'Copy that. Missile is released.'

'Confirm estimated time of impact?'

'Ten seconds, and counting…'

CHAPTER FIFTY-TWO

Algeria

'Get down!'

Nathan grabbed Eva's sleeve and pulled her to the floor.

She swore as her elbow smacked against the hard earth, then Decker shoved his hand against her and tumbled on top of them both.

Just in time.

She felt the shockwave a split second before the roar from the explosion hit her, dust and stones cascading over her head and shoulders.

Hot metal fragments shot overhead, and her eyes widened as a long piece of metal embedded itself in the wooden doorframe.

'Stay down.'

Decker's hand met the back of her head at the same time as his voice, and she gritted her teeth as a secondary explosion ripped through the hot air.

'Fuel tanks,' mumbled Nathan.

As a cloud of sand passed overhead, Eva blinked and used her arm to shield her face.

Her ears were ringing, her eyes were streaming, and she turned away for a moment to spit out the dirt that had somehow found its way around her teeth.

'Fucking hell,' said Decker.

Eva wiped at her eyes, then raised her head to see the older assassin peering around the stone wall, his expression grim.

Following his gaze, she pushed her fringe out of the way and blinked.

She had never seen a MQ-9 Reaper up close, never realised how alien the aircraft appeared with its windowless nose cone and fuselage.

'They must've caught him hovering a few miles away,' said Nathan. 'They were supposed to make sure it crashed into the hills, not here.'

'Bloody spooks,' said Decker.

The drone had crashed on its belly, skidding past the crater where Leavey's Land Rover had once stood, and buried itself into the earth only a few hundred metres away from their position.

Black smoke rose from the broken aircraft, flames

spewing from the pierced fuel tank while the stench of burning plastic and metal assaulted Eva's senses.

Decker shielded his eyes with a hand. 'Well, at least no-one will fly that thing again.'

'A shame someone didn't take care of it properly the first time around,' said Nathan. He frowned as his phone started to ring, then put it on speaker. 'Miles?'

'Everyone all right?'

'Yes,' said Eva. 'On our way out of here now. We should be across the border and back in Tangier tonight.'

'Change of plan.'

She bit her lip at the sound of Knox's voice, saw Decker roll his eyes, then shook her head to silence him as he opened his mouth.

'What's going on?' she said.

'We've received new intelligence to suggest Elliott Wilder's private plane has lodged a flight plan to Monaco. Not only that, we've discovered that he hasn't been working alone. He has a brother – Aaron Sykes.'

'The financier that brokers deals for foreign governments?' said Nathan. 'But he's Romanian, not English.'

'Elliott Wilder had two siblings,' said Miles. 'They didn't travel to the UK with their parents when they left in the sixties and were raised by an uncle in Bucharest.'

'Why the bloody hell did we not know this before?' said Decker.

'We only got confirmation a few minutes ago from our sources there,' said Knox. 'And we need to move fast on the information, because when Elliott finds out his drone's been destroyed and his plan to start a new war in Turkey and the Middle East has gone with it, we think he'll make a run for it.'

'To Russia?' said Eva.

'Quite possibly.'

'Hang on,' said Nathan. 'You said Elliott had two siblings. Who's the other one?'

Eva heard the Section chief sigh, a mixture of exasperation and frustration in his next words.

'Charlotte Hughes. Private Secretary to Edward Toskins, Minister for the Department for International Trade.'

'Fuck me,' said Decker, shaking his head.

'All three are Russian agents,' said Miles. 'And between them, they've managed to embed themselves in deep cover for the past fifteen years. God knows what secrets they've managed to hand over to their masters in Moscow. We've also received an anonymous tip-off from Prague with the toxicology reports on the poisoned dart that killed Kelly O'Hara. It contained traces of a Russian-designed nerve agent, as well as an anti-coagulant.'

'The PM wants this contained, and now,' said Knox. 'That means no-one else can be involved, so we need you back here. Your mission is to remove Elliott Wilder and his immediate family. Cut them off from him so he has nowhere else to go. Permanently. Is that understood?'

'Understood,' said Decker. 'Anything else?'

'Try to be subtle about it.'

Eva ended the call, already calculating how far the small car had travelled, and how much fuel they had left.

It would be close.

'Okay, let's get on with this,' she said, setting her shoulders.

'Are you serious?' said Nathan, his eyes wide. 'We've just spent the best part of three years keeping our heads down and avoiding the Section. Now you want to go back?'

'It's like Knox said. We're the only ones who can do this covertly – otherwise it'll be all-out war in the government, let alone everywhere else.' She sighed. 'And, let's face it – if anyone else gets the job, our chances of getting a reprieve are over.'

'Let them deal with it,' he said, his eyes pleading. 'I thought we were going to have a quiet life.'

'No chance of that. Have you seen the crater over there?' said Eva. 'That'll be all over the US Geological Survey website by now. The minute they realise that wasn't a seismic event, this place will be crawling. We've got to get out of here.'

Nathan blinked weary eyes, then shrugged. 'All right. Lead the way.'

Eva swung her bag over her shoulder and frowned. Decker was peering at his phone screen, the maps app open. 'Decker? Come on. We need to go – now.'

He looked up, then shook his head. 'You go to London. It's too cold for me. I'll get a lift with you to Tangier, then I'm out of here.'

'Where are you going?' said Nathan.

Decker shot him a wicked grin and held up his phone with the weather app displayed. 'Monaco. Much warmer.'

CHAPTER FIFTY-THREE

London

Eva removed the motorcycle helmet, shook out her hair, and peered across the darkened street at a row of Georgian terraced houses lining the avenue.

Ornate street lamps cast a dappled light through sycamore tree branches, a slight breeze rocking the boughs above her head.

In the distance, the sound of a city settling into evening carried through the suburbs, the rush of traffic on the nearby A-road easing into white noise.

'Aaron Sykes – Elliott's brother – owns the house on the end, where the cobblestones start,' said Nathan under his breath. 'He rents it out to Charlotte via a shell company. He arrived with Elliott in a private jet earlier this week. Elliott returned to France while Aaron stayed behind at his other house in Pimlico.'

'What's he doing in London?'

'Whatever Elliott tells him to, according to Miles.' Nathan took the helmet from her and stashed it in a pannier, then removed a 9mm pistol and handed it over. 'This morning, Aaron met with one of the government's suppliers – the managing director of that company is currently being interviewed by MI6 about possible terrorism charges.'

'They didn't arrest him?'

'They wanted to keep the ruse going, that he wasn't under suspicion until everyone was ready.'

Eva reached inside her leather jacket and attached a suppressor to the pistol before tucking it back inside. 'What about Charlotte?'

'Worked her way up through the admin ranks.'

'And no-one notices a secretary, right?' She sighed. 'God knows how many secrets she's managed to pass on over the years. Jeffrey's espionage skills must've been getting rusty if he didn't figure out what she was up to.'

'Or maybe he was simply too focused on stopping Elliott Wilder and his Turkish clients to realise.'

'I suppose. Right, I'm out of here.'

'Stay safe.'

'Always.'

Eva shoved her hands into the pockets of her jacket and crossed the street, edging closer towards her target.

She paused, huddling against a privet hedge in desperate need of a trim, and bit back a sneeze – the sudden change in climate from the desert to a rain-soaked Finsbury Park had taken its toll on her already exhausted body, but she couldn't afford to be seen.

Get in.

Get the job done.

Get out.

'Just like the old days,' she muttered.

'Didn't catch that,' said a voice in her ear.

'Nothing. Thinking aloud, that's all.' She glanced over her shoulder to where Nathan sat waiting on the motorbike, and toggled her lapel microphone. 'Any sign of her?'

'She's inside, in the living room.'

'What's the latest on Aaron?'

'He's still at home in Pimlico. MI6 has a watching brief on his flat, and the lights in the living area and kitchen are on. No movement to report.'

Eva turned away from the bike and started walking towards her target's building, a fine mist distorting the glow from the streetlights above her head, the promise of more rain lending an ozone-heavy scent to the air.

Up ahead, the car-lined street was quiet and as she craned her neck to peer into ground-floor flats she could see televisions playing, the residents oblivious to the assassin who passed their front doors.

A few metres from the building, she frowned and

ducked into an alleyway, cupping her hand around her lapel microphone.

'Nathan – did they manage to get inside before Aaron arrived back earlier?'

'No – too many neighbours around working from home, so they have no cameras or microphones in place. They have directional microphones at the windows though.' Nathan wrinkled his nose. 'He's playing opera.'

'Shit.' Eva closed her eyes, then took a deep breath. 'So how do they know he's inside?'

'What?'

'How do they know he's inside? They can't hear anything except opera music, they have no cameras in situ. Who's covering the fire exits and roof?'

'Hang on. I'll ask.'

'Jesus.' She slipped into the shadows of a brick wall bordering one side of the alley, wrinkling her nose at the stench of dog shit, and checked over her shoulder.

No-one approached, and she could hear no footsteps.

Only the sound of her heartbeat in her ears, matching the tight sensation clutching at her chest.

'Eva?'

She blinked in surprise at Miles's voice in her ear.

'They've lost him, haven't they?' she said, unable to keep the disgust from her voice.

'It's a complete cock-up,' he said. 'There's a fire exit in the hallway beside his bedroom. No-one saw him go out the window up it. We assume he's escaped across the roof and down another fire escape to a car park behind one of the properties further along the street. Elliott must've warned him.'

'Shit.'

'What about aerial reconnaissance?' said Nathan. 'Infra-red.'

'Probably too late,' said the Section manager. 'We're issuing an all-ports alert for him, but whether it reaches the right people in time...'

'Miles? We have to stop Aaron from leaving the country,' said Eva. 'If we don't, he's going to head somewhere you can't extradite him from. I would.'

There was a brief moment of silence, then, 'Leave it with me. Where are you?'

'A couple of miles away from headquarters. I've got a house call to make.'

'Report back in when you're done.'

She cursed under her breath. 'If you want a job doing properly...'

'You can't be in two places at once,' said Nathan. 'Let them go after Aaron.'

'We should've killed him first.'

'Concentrate, Eva. If Elliott's warned his brother, then chances are Charlotte is ready to leave as well.'

'I'm on my way.'

She ran the remainder of the route, urgency in her long strides before reaching the building.

Taking a moment to step back, she raised her gaze to the windows above.

Charlotte's flat was two storeys up, and Eva could see a soft glow emanating through the gaps around the drawn curtains.

Moving to the front door, she paused.

A chink of light shone through a gap where it had been propped open.

Exhaling, trying to lose the effect of the adrenalin rush, she pushed it open to see a man in his thirties wheeling a bicycle towards her, his eyes widening in surprise at her sudden entry.

Eva's eyes fell to the hospital ID card pinned to his shirt.

'Sorry.' She smiled. 'Urgent delivery for Charlotte Hughes. You know what it's like with us government workers. Flat—'

'Six. Upstairs, on the left.'

'Thanks.' Eva held open the door for him. 'Have a good shift.'

He grinned. 'You too.'

Closing the door, she thumbed off the safety switch on her weapon and then hurried the length of the hallway.

There was no lift in the building, and the fire exit door remained closed beside what turned out to be a cleaner's store cupboard.

Eva peered through the reinforced glass window in

the door.

Stairs went upwards, but no further down – the emergency exit from the building appeared to be a secure door on the other side of the glass, leading out the back of the building.

'Nathan? Get yourself over here,' she murmured. 'I need you to watch the back door for me. We don't need a repeat mistake.'

'Copy that.'

Toggling off the microphone, Eva moved back to the main staircase and crept upwards.

She paused at the landing, crossed the hallway checking the numbers of the flats she passed, then moved on.

At the top of the second flight, she swung her gun around to her right.

Flat six was in front of her.

She ran through the layout in her mind, memorised from plans that Nathan had found on the borough council's database from the original redevelopment over twenty years ago and updated after Miles and Emily's search efforts.

Raising her hand, she knocked twice and moved away from the spy-hole.

A moment later, she heard footsteps approach across what sounded like a laminate flooring. No heels – a softer tone.

Running shoes, perhaps.

'Who is it?'

Eva didn't respond.

Two things could happen next.

First, the occupier of the flat would walk away, thinking she'd made a mistake and no-one was at the door.

Second, curiosity would set in, and the door would open.

She held her breath.

Behind the wooden surface, she heard the scrape of a chain being removed.

Then a bolt slid back into its housing.

After that, she heard a lock being turned.

A split second later, the door began to open.

Eva elbowed her way in, kicked it closed and held her gun steady.

A woman held up her hands, her eyes open in shock and surprise.

Charlotte Hughes.

'Move.' Eva used the gun to indicate the living room before it found its target once more.

Soft music played in the background and as Eva followed the woman, she noticed an open door to her right and risked a quick glance inside.

An open suitcase lay on the bed, and the wardrobe doors had been flung open with clothes tossed onto the floor or over a wooden chair beside an antique dressing table.

'Going somewhere in a hurry?' she said as they reached the open plan living space.

The flat still bore the effect of Miles and Emily's break-in, with books and magazines strewn across the floor and a pile of crystal glass swept to one side of the kitchen tiles.

The music fell silent and she bit back a curse.

No matter – this far away from the front door, no-one would hear the suppressed gunshot and with any luck the neighbours would be engrossed in their own lives, too busy to realise a Russian spy had been living next door all this time.

'I can pay you,' said Charlotte. She turned when she reached the kitchen worktop, rested her hands either side and used her forefinger to rub at an imagined stain on the counter. 'Whatever it is your masters are paying you, we can offer more.'

'Thanks, but no thanks. Where's Aaron?'

The woman held up her phone, and smirked. 'You're too late. He's already gone.'

'And he didn't wait for you?' Eva raised an eyebrow. 'So much for family loyalty.'

'Shut up.'

Eva jabbed her thumb over her shoulder. 'So what's that in there? Did you change your mind at the last minute? Decide against going home after all?'

'What's it to you?'

'Just curious, that's all.' Eva blinked, a realisation

striking her the next second. 'Shit, he never came to collect you, did he? He knew we were watching his flat and decided to get out of the country while he could.'

'That's not true.'

Eva laughed. 'It is, isn't it. How long were you going to give him? Another hour? Two?'

Charlotte crossed her arms over her chest. 'It doesn't matter. By the time your lot catch up with him, he'll be on his way to Russia. And you will have failed.'

'I don't think so,' Eva snarled, then raised the gun.

It coughed twice, the shots hitting their target centre mass, and Charlotte Hughes slumped to the floor, the kitchen cupboards speckled with her blood.

'One down, two to go,' muttered Eva, then turned on her heel and sprinted for the door.

CHAPTER FIFTY-FOUR

Monaco

Elliott removed the cigar from his mouth and blew a tendril of sweet smoke into the night air, exhaling some of the stress that had wracked his body for weeks.

The adrenalin rush of the negotiations with Yilmaz was starting to fade, and his attention would soon be taken by new opportunities.

New threats.

New wars.

A satisfied smile accompanied a relaxing of his shoulders.

All in good time.

For now, he eyed the twinkling harbour lights below the villa's landscaped gardens and waited patiently for the phone to ring while he watched the dip and rise of planes at the airport across the water.

A sea breeze whispered against his cheeks, and he inhaled the salty air before taking another drag on the cigar.

He would call the accountant in the morning.

The General's money had landed in the bank account at the same time Elliott had left Turkish airspace. There were investments to make, palms to grease, bribes to make.

All the mechanisations of a busy arms dealership that was going from strength to strength.

A buzzing noise jolted him from his thoughts, and he wandered back inside.

Reaching his desk, he noticed the General's number on the screen display and frowned.

'General?'

'Your fucking shipment never arrived,' Yilmaz hissed, his accent thick with anger. 'The British intercepted it in Malta. You owe me four missiles, and more.'

Elliott pulled an ashtray closer, then crushed out the cigar. 'I'm afraid I cannot help you, Yilmaz. The contract has been signed and the money exchanged – the risk became yours over twenty-four hours ago, not mine.'

'You have betrayed me. The drone is missing, too.'

'What? Where?'

'After you left the warehouse, my men lost contact with it. What did you do?'

Elliott frowned as he processed the other man's words. 'General, I can assure you that was nothing to do with me. Are you sure your men were capable pilots?'

'You have double-crossed me, Mr Wilder,' the General spat. 'You have, in all likelihood, taken back the drone in order to sell it to someone else now that you have my money.'

'Be careful, General. I have very little time for people who besmirch my good character. Remember who you're talking to.'

'Are you threatening me?'

'Yes, General, I am,' Elliott sneered. 'I can always report your planned insurgency to my contacts within the Turkish embassy in London who, I'm sure, would be very interested to hear about your planned coup. Do you think your family will survive that? Do you think anyone would find your bodies?'

The line went silent.

'General, are you still there?'

'You will pay for this, Mr Wilder,' Yilmaz hissed.

'I very much doubt it, General. Goodbye.' Elliott ended the call, then exhaled as a second number appeared on the screen and answered.

'It's me,' said a familiar voice.

Finally, the call he expected – hoped – would come.

'Are you at the airport?'

'I'm at the departure gate. Anything from Charlotte?'

'No answer, yet.'

'The plane leaves in thirty minutes.'

'You must go without her, if necessary.'

'What do I tell them when I get there?' said Aaron. 'They won't be happy that we failed.'

Elliott chuckled. 'Do not worry. You have caused enough chaos within the British government over the years to keep them happy. There are other missions. We're not the only ones. Expect a debriefing, that is all.'

His brother lowered his voice. 'They won't let me leave again, will they?'

'I doubt it.' He sighed. 'We knew it could come to this. Make the most of it – buy a nice dacha outside Moscow. Paint, like you used to when we were children. Enjoy life.'

'And you?'

Elliott eyed the paperwork strewn across the desk, his gaze moving to the gaping maw of the safe he'd emptied an hour ago, the two canvas bags zipped closed on the hearth rug beside a smouldering fire that had been allowed to die.

'I will make my own way home.' He rolled his shoulders, cricked his neck as he paced towards the windows and took in the view once more. 'I shall miss the scenery, Aaron.'

'A small sacrifice to make in return for your life.'

His brother paused as his voice was drowned out by an announcement. 'They will start boarding in twenty minutes.'

'Then, go.' He checked his watch. 'You'll land in about nine hours. I'll call you with an update.'

'I'll be waiting.'

'I must go. There is another call coming through – it's her.' Elliott rested his hand on the patio door frame as he put the phone to his ear once more. 'Charlotte?'

She didn't reply, and he could only hear a soft breathing at the end of the line.

'Charlotte?'

'Charlotte is dead.'

He swallowed, his dry throat rasping. 'Who is this?'

'My name is Eva Delacourt.'

'You will live to regret this, I swear it,' he sneered. 'No-one does this to my family. No-one—'

'Elliott?'

'What?'

'Shut the fuck up, and look behind you.'

Heart racing, his jaw set, he did as the woman told him.

Fury turned to disbelief, then fear.

A tall figure leaned against the open patio doors, black T-shirt over worn jeans, bare arms tanned and strong – and pointing a gun straight at him.

'Who the hell—'

The shot hit him in the chest.

Elliott dropped the phone, the blast knocking him backwards.

His head smacked against the marble floor tiles, a dreadful pain coursing through his chest as his lungs tried to find air, instead drowning in blood.

He heard the woman's voice call out from the discarded phone as the assassin stood over him and took aim at his left eye.

'That's two down, Decker. One more to go.'

CHAPTER FIFTY-FIVE

London

'How the fuck did he get through security?'

Miles tried to shake off a creeping sense of exhaustion as Gerald Knox stalked the floor, the Section chief's face flushed with anger.

'The all-ports advice reached the security team at customs too late to stop him,' he said. 'We've lost the advantage here, Gerald, but we still have ten minutes until that plane is due to take off.'

'They won't ground it without a bloody good reason,' Knox said. He paused beside the analysts who kept their gaze resolutely on their computer screens. 'Given the debacle with customs, we can't guarantee that the message will get through to the pilot in time, either. It's not as if we can launch a couple of fighter planes to intercept it over the North Sea without the media having a field day either, is it?'

Miles frowned, turned away from the Section chief, and crossed the room to where Greg sat. 'Where is Marie Weston right now?'

'Upstairs.'

'Get hold of her, and tell her we need her down here – now.'

'Will do.'

'And what about our drone? Where's that?'

'Currently flying a mission over the northern coast of France.' Greg cleared his throat. 'I can't say more than that.'

'Active mission, or reconnaissance?' said Knox.

The analyst squirmed in his chair. 'Reconnaissance, I believe, Chief.'

Knox's gaze met Miles's, and a smile formed on his lips. 'If you're thinking what I think you're thinking, Newcombe—'

'We'll worry about the arguments and the paperwork afterwards,' said Miles. 'Greg, tell them to turn back. We need them over Heathrow – immediately.'

'We nearly didn't get away with it last time,' said Knox.

'Do you have any other ideas, given that Aaron's plane is about to take off?'

'No.' Knox turned his attention to the door as the security panel buzzed, and Nathan's sister walked in.

'You asked for me, Chief?'

'Marie, we need your skills as co-pilot.' Knox gestured to a spare seat beside a computer. 'Our drone pilot is online, but his intelligence officer is dealing with another matter – you'll need to guide him in for us and make sure we stay clear of radar until we can clear this up with the MoD, understand?'

'Copy that,' she said, and swung herself into the chair.

'Your job is to stay within Heathrow's airspace so that flight to Moscow isn't allowed to take off,' continued the Section chief, 'and make sure you keep a look out for the RAF. I've sent a message to RAF Waddington about what we're doing and why but just in case—'

'Will it work? Will they ground the aircraft?' said Emily, peering over her shoulder.

Miles winked. 'Just don't tell anyone. Most people still think that the last time at Gatwick was a suspected terrorist incident.'

A rapid string of commands filled the room as Marie and the team of analysts exchanged data, and then the screens in front of Miles flickered once before the drone's cameras provided a view of the Sussex countryside.

'Thank Christ it's dark,' said Knox under his breath.

'I'd hate to have to explain this one to the general public.'

'With any luck, we'll be able to field any local enquiries without raising suspicion,' said Miles.

'I hope so.' Knox frowned. 'And where the hell are Delacourt and Newcombe?'

Miles glanced at his watch. 'Well, Eva should be boarding that plane bound for Moscow about now.'

CHAPTER FIFTY-SIX

Heathrow

Eva smoothed down the ill-fitting skirt and smiled at the final stream of passengers entering through the door in the fuselage of the airliner.

The navy uniform held a tangible whiff of expensive perfume, the bemused former owner now wearing a high visibility vest over black trousers and a sweatshirt while she stood on the gangway and pretended to check through the passenger manifest and catering paperwork with a colleague.

Eva's heart was still racing from the motorbike journey across London to the busy international airport.

She hadn't taken Crowe for a motorcyclist – they hadn't used one in Prague – but he flew along the motorway like a man possessed, only braking once they reached the security gates and were let through onto the concourse beneath the passenger terminals.

The team at headquarters were still arguing with their counterparts in government about what to do with Aaron Sykes, but Knox's orders were still ringing in her ears from the day before.

The Prime Minister wanted Elliott Wilder and his siblings dealt with – permanently.

Unless and until she heard otherwise, Eva planned to do just that.

She blinked, then forced another smile while she listened to the stewardess at her elbow murmuring directions to passengers and doing her best to cover for Eva's non-existent knowledge of the aircraft's seating arrangements.

The last stragglers boarded with apologies, duty-free purchases and alcohol-laden breath before being ushered to their places in economy class by a patient steward. Final checks were made, and the door was closed while the staff disbanded to settle in their customers for the eight-and-a-half-hour flight to Moscow.

Eva pulled out her phone, cursing under her breath at the screen.

No missed calls.

Peering through the window to the concrete apron

below, she spotted Nathan standing beside a thickset man with a walkie-talkie radio.

The taller man held up his hands.

No news yet.

'Dammit, Crowe.' Eva straightened and watched as two stewardesses worked in the tiny galley beside her. 'I don't fancy my chances in Russia.'

The crew hadn't been told why she had joined them at the last minute, simply that her presence was linked to a security matter and that they were to await further instructions.

In the meantime, she had work to do.

A commotion past the open door to the cockpit caught her attention, and she strained to listen over the excited murmurs of the cabin crew beside her.

'What's going on?' she said, impatient.

The woman next to her, whose badge identified her as the cabin services director, gave an exasperated sigh.

'The whole airport is closing. There's been an unidentified craft in the area, so they're not letting any aircraft land – or take off. We're stuck here until they sort it out.'

A groan arose from the three staff members hovering at the galley while Eva battened down the adrenalin flowing through her.

'Best thing to do is keep the passengers happy while we wait for further instructions,' the woman continued. 'Come on, you all know what to do.'

Eva shot one of the stewardesses a thankful smile as she handed her a glass of champagne, then moved up the staircase towards the first class lounge.

Loosening the red scarf at her neck, she reached into her bra and pulled out a tiny yellow pill before dropping it into the drink.

She swirled it around, careful not to spill any of the liquid on her skin, and then lifted her chin as she reached the upper deck.

Despite the captain's voice ringing out over the intercom explaining there would be a short delay, the atmosphere was calmer up here, a different ambience to the cramped and noisy conditions in the lower class cabins below.

Only half a dozen passengers were on the top deck, strategically placed by the crew so that they didn't encroach on each other's privacy.

She spotted Aaron Sykes towards the rear of the cabin, his face turned to the window as he tapped an empty bottle of water on his knee.

Eva frowned, did a quick calculation and then relaxed.

He wouldn't be able to see Nathan from here, wouldn't be able to see the armed personnel who hovered in the shadows in case Elliott Wilder's brother tried to flee.

She set her shoulders and a smile on her face as she drew closer.

Bending down, she cleared her throat.

'Mr Sykes, a glass of champagne – courtesy of the airline to ease the inconvenience of our current situation.'

Her earpiece hissed to life, the noise a painful jolt, and she shook her head, unnerved by the sudden voice in her ear.

'Eva? They've grounded all aircraft,' Nathan said. 'Unidentified aircraft spotted above Heathrow. All flights in and out of London are being diverted. Stand down.'

Aaron's eyes widened.

'Delacourt,' he sneered.

Eva took a step back, unable to conceal her surprise. 'How do you—'

Too late.

Aaron Sykes unclipped his seatbelt, and swept the champagne glass from her grasp with his hand before she could react.

The poisoned drink spilled over the carpet, showering the side of the seats opposite and splattering up the side of the cabin.

'Fuck,' Eva hissed.

She lashed out with the heel of her hand, catching Sykes under his chin as he advanced towards her, then used her other hand to chop at his windpipe.

He crashed to the floor gasping, unable to avoid her foot as it connected with his jaw.

'Eva?'

Nathan's voice carried through the raging noise of her heartbeat in her ears and she paused, her hands resting on the back of the seat as she tried to work out whether there was enough poison left at the bottom of the champagne flute rolling across the carpet or whether she would have to throttle the Russian agent.

'What?'

'The Prime Minister's changed her mind. Knox says she wants Aaron Sykes alive. Apparently it'll give her some leverage with the rest of her party colleagues.'

Eva nudged Sykes's leg with the toe of her shoe as he smirked at her, then reached under her uniform jacket for her gun.

The man's eyes widened as she caressed her finger across the trigger.

The suppressed gunfire echoed off the fuselage, mixing with the screams of shocked passengers who scrambled out of their seats and onto the floor.

Lowering the weapon, Eva contemplated the gaping hole in the Russian spy's forehead and smiled.

'Oops.'

CHAPTER FIFTY-SEVEN

Four days later

Eva stood behind a large Doric pillar beside the steps leading out of the small church in Piccadilly and squinted at a grey and overcast sky as a light drizzle prickled her umbrella, the wind snapping at the nylon material.

At the kerbside, three black four-door vehicles stood with engines purring, uniformed drivers helping passengers into the back seats before the doors were slammed and the cars eased into the traffic.

She watched as they disappeared around a corner, then sighed and turned to the man beside her.

'That was different.'

'As memorials go, I suppose it had to be subtle,'

said Nathan, pulling his black tie away from his collar. 'They were never going to do anything else.'

'I suppose.' She ran her thumb over the order of service, tracing the names of Patrick Leavey, Adrian Ogilvy and Jeffrey Dukes. 'At least Knox was able to say a few words.'

'But no-one will ever know the truth,' said Nathan. 'No-one will know how close Elliott Wilder got to starting a coup in Turkey and another war in the Middle East, or how those three men helped to prevent it happening.'

'*We'll* know,' said Eva, 'and so will everyone else involved in this. They won't be forgotten. That's what matters.'

Nathan held out his hand. 'The rain's stopped. Fancy a drink somewhere before we head back to Prague?'

'Go on, then. I spotted a bar that looked quiet for this time of day just along the road on our way here.'

She lowered her umbrella, slipped her hand through his arm and fell into step beside him.

'Any news from Knox about the charges the PM wanted to press after you shot Sykes? MI6 were keen to speak to him, weren't they?'

'I managed to convince them it was an accident. My hands were sweaty – my finger slipped.'

'Did they believe you?'

'I don't think so.' Eva grimaced. 'But I think I'm

forgiven. Knox mentioned something about there being one less terrorist to worry about.'

Nathan shook his head as they turned into a busy four-lane street and crossed it, dodging between taxis and double-decker buses before pointing to the sign for the bar.

'What do you want to do after all this, Eva?' he said, turning to her before they reached the doorway.

'I don't know.' She smiled. 'Actually, I do. I want a long soak in a hot bath. I want to find a beach somewhere without a phone signal, and I want to sleep.'

'Fancy something to eat first?' he said. He stopped and pulled her to one side as he took out his mobile phone, and thumbed the screen lock.

'Yes, I do,' she said. 'Who're you phoning?'

'Decker. We'd better let him know the news, right?' Eva grinned as the video call was answered.

'Hang on.'

She glanced at Nathan while Decker spoke to someone in Spanish, then turned down the volume on the speakerphone as the shouting on the other end got louder.

'Where the hell are you?' she said.

'El Salvador.'

'What happened about going back to Italy after all this was over?' said Nathan. 'I thought you said you had work to do on the farm?'

'Change of plan. Make it quick – things are about to kick off here.'

'Thought you might like to know that the Prime Minister has granted us all amnesty. We're no longer wanted by the British government.'

Decker chuckled. 'Well, at least that's one less target on my back.'

'What?' said Nathan, his eyes widening. 'Who else wants you dead?'

'Too many to—' He broke off and spoke to someone in the background before shots rang out and his attention returned to the screen. 'I've got to go. Shout if you need me.'

'Thanks, Decker,' said Eva. She reached out and ended the call, then buttoned her jacket as a cold wind whipped along the street and tugged at her hair.

'Was that gunfire?' said Nathan, his eyes wide. 'What the hell is he doing in Central America?'

'God knows.' Eva wound her fingers around his hand and led him towards the bar.

'Do you think he'll be all right?'

'It sounded to me like he was having a blast. I don't think we have to worry about him,' said Eva, and raised her gaze to the sky at a sorrowful cry.

A gull soared on the breeze, its movements hypnotic as it rose and fell on the air currents.

Nathan moved closer and gave her a nudge with his

elbow. 'You've been a bit quiet since we were debriefed. What's wrong?'

'Nothing.'

'Bullshit. Come on – this is me you're talking to.'

She peered over her shoulder as the door to the bar opened and voices filtered out ahead of the small crowd that spilled out onto the pavement, their voices buoyant, then turned back to him.

'A drone, Crowe. They used a drone to stop Aaron's flight taking off in the end. They were prepared to do that, instead of letting me deal with him. Like I'm trained to do.'

'Well, I suppose it's like Miles said in the debriefing. Cutting edge technology, and all that.'

Eva sighed and shielded her eyes with her hand as she gazed at the clouds scudding across the sky.

'Bloody drones. I'm going to be out of a job at this rate.'

THE END

ABOUT THE AUTHOR

Before turning to writing, *USA Today* bestselling author Rachel Amphlett played guitar in bands, dabbled in radio as a presenter and freelance producer for the BBC, and worked in publishing as an editorial assistant.

She now wields a pen instead of a plectrum and writes crime fiction and spy thrillers, including the fast paced *Dan Taylor* and *English Assassins* spy thrillers, and the *Detective Kay Hunter* and *Detective Mark Turpin* mysteries.

After 13 years in Australia, Rachel is currently based in the UK.

You can find out more about her writing and visit her online shop at www.rachelamphlett.com.

Printed in Great Britain
by Amazon